Anonymous

The Battle worth fighting

And other Stories

Anonymous

The Battle worth fighting
And other Stories

ISBN/EAN: 9783337148430

Printed in Europe, USA, Canada, Australia, Japan

Cover: Foto ©Andreas Hilbeck / pixelio.de

More available books at **www.hansebooks.com**

THE
BATTLE WORTH FIGHTING.

THE

BATTLE WORTH FIGHTING;

AND OTHER STORIES.

PUBLISHED UNDER THE DIRECTION OF
THE COMMITTEE OF GENERAL LITERATURE AND EDUCATION ;
APPOINTED BY THE SOCIETY FOR PROMOTING
CHRISTIAN KNOWLEDGE.

LONDON:
SOCIETY FOR PROMOTING CHRISTIAN KNOWLEDGE;
SOLD AT THE DEPOSITORIES:
77, GREAT QUEEN STREET, LINCOLN'S INN FIELDS ;
4, ROYAL EXCHANGE ; 48, PICCADILLY ;
AND BY ALL BOOKSELLERS.

LONDON :

R. CLAY, SON, AND TAYLOR, PRINTERS,

BREAD STREET HILL.

CONTENTS.

BATTLE WORTH FIGHTING.

"He that is slow to anger is better than the mighty; and he
that ruleth his spirit than he that taketh a city."—Prov.
xvi. 32.

A LITTLE party of students sat round a table which was
well covered with books and slates. At one end were
three boys of about the same age; at the other two little
girls; and between them a boy of seven or eight—a
new comer, who had taken his place at their table, that
day, for the first time. A little apart, in the pleasant
bow-window, sat the master, Dr. Hale, amusing himself, by turns, with a newspaper, and two or three
groups loitering in the quiet Close, on their way homewards from the afternoon service at the Cathedral. The
little girls were his daughters; the four boys his
pupils.

"Norry," whispered Mary Hale, the elder and more
staid-looking of the two sisters, "you are not doing
your sum."

"No, my pencil won't mark. Will you cut it for
me?"

"I haven't any penknife. Go and ask Robert Warner, the boy who is putting up his writing-case."

Norry stared very doubtfully at Robert, who certainly

was the least pleasant-looking of the three boys at the other end of the table.

"I don't think he'll do it," said Norry, bringing his eyes slowly back to Mary's face again.

"Then try some one else."

Norry slid down from his high chair, and stationing himself behind Arthur Clayton, the handsomest of the three boys, asked him, very humbly, if he would cut his pencil.

"Do what?" said Arthur, with an abruptness that rather startled Norry—"cut your pencil? Why can't you cut it for yourself?"

"I haven't any penknife."

"Then borrow one."

A handsome knife was lying before Arthur, but he did not offer to lend it.

"Here," said the boy next to him, "you may have mine."

Norry took the knife, but handled it so awkwardly that the point of his pencil was broken more than once. At the third failure Robert Warner stretched across the table for the pencil, made a neat point to it, and told Norry he was to take it to him the next time it wanted cutting.

When he got back to his place Mary Hale was putting up her books, and she told Norry the sum had better be left for the next day.

In a few minutes the table was cleared, and only two big boys, Robert and Arthur, lingered in the room, each having a few lines of Virgil to recite as a punishment for misconduct that morning during Dr. Hale's absence. Robert went through his task very steadily ; but Arthur was ill-prepared with his, and made so many blunders that the lesson was returned before he had got half through it.

" And now Arthur," said Dr. Hale, when the book was at last closed, "as you admitted you were the aggressor to-day, I hope you are willing to apologise to Robert."

" I would rather not, sir," answered Arthur, flushing.

" Why not ?"

" It is not pleasant, sir."

" Certainly not, but the same thing may be said of a great many of the duties we owe to each other. Do you think that any excuse for leaving them undone ?"

" I don't know, sir ; perhaps not when they're *only* unpleasant."

" Then you think this is something more ?"

" Yes, sir," answered Arthur, after a moment's hesitation ; " it isn't manly."

" Not manly to acknowledge oneself in the wrong ! I should like to hear your notion of manliness, Arthur."

But Arthur was not ready with a definition, so, after waiting a minute very patiently, Dr. Hale said, " Well, if you cannot define what you mean, give me an example."

" Alexander, sir, or Napoleon," returned Arthur, promptly.

" In what did their manliness consist ?"

" In what, sir ? Why, they were great conquerors !"

" And great slaves at the same time."

" How do you mean, sir ?"

" Why, slaves to their passions, which are the worst

things that can rule a man. Have you ever read the life of Alexander carefully, especially the latter part?"

"Yes, sir; he had some vices, I know, so has everybody."

"No doubt; but the true heroes are they who conquer them, or, at least try hard to do so. The Bible says, 'He that hath no rule over his own spirit is like a city that is broken down, and without walls.' Can you picture anything more utterly lost and desolate? And again, 'He that is slow to anger is better than the mighty.' Did you ever try to get a victory over yourself, Arthur?—over your temper for instance?"

"No, sir, I don't think I ever did."

"Then you cannot tell how difficult it is, and what a great amount of manliness it calls into action. Suppose you make a first attempt now, Arthur, and beg Robert's pardon for what you feel was amiss in your conduct to him this morning?"

But Arthur evinced no readiness to take Dr. Hale's advice. He hung back with an angry frown darkening his clear forehead and bright blue eyes. At last Robert generously came to his relief.

"Perhaps, as you didn't see what passed this morning, sir, you'll excuse him," he said.

"Certainly, I've no wish to force him, but I should be glad to see him choose the right course for himself. Well, now you may go, boys."

Arthur availed himself at once of the permission, but Robert lingered to ask if he might go out that evening.

"To Nunstead, I suppose," said Dr. Hale.

" Yes, sir."

" Very well, you'll have two hours' light if you start directly after tea. How are you getting on ?"

" Not very fast, sir. I'll show you what I've done."

Robert produced from a small folio half a dozen sketches, and spread them carefully out on Dr. Hale's table. They were in different stages of progress, but seemed much alike in other respects; the subject of each being an old ivy-covered house.

" I see nothing amiss in them," said Dr. Hale, taking up the two most finished ones. "They are beautiful sketches."

" But do they give you a good idea of the place, sir ?"

" Yes, as it is now, but there was less ivy round this side of the house in your mother's time."

" Will you mark out how far it reached, sir ?" said Robert, taking up a pencil.

" And spoil your drawing ?"

" No sir, it will do it no harm."

Dr. Hale used the pencil as lightly as possible, and mentioned one or two other points in which the aspect of the house and grounds differed from what it was twenty years ago. Then the sketches were put away, and a few drawing materials collected to be ready for use as soon as tea was over.

About half an hour after, Robert was back in the study again, but he found Mary Hale and Norry there before him.

" Mamma says we may go with you, Robert," she said ; " you won't mind taking Norry, will you ?"

" Not if you can walk fast."

Norry not only undertook to do that, but to run if required ; so the three children set off together, and Norry, in his anxiety to be as good as his word, generally contrived to keep a little ahead of the other two. Their walk was a very pleasant one ; first through the quiet Close, and then out by some sheltered lanes into the open fields. There Norry found it a little difficult to pass the fresh hedge flowers, but whenever he stopped to look at them, the sight of Mary and Robert, coming on behind with grave business-like faces, sent him trotting off faster than ever. At last some straggling cottages were passed ; then they turned into a quiet churchyard, and Norry was told that he might rest himself, for they were not going any further. So he sat down with Mary on one of the little grassy mounds, and Robert walked about, always keeping his eyes steadily fixed on the old grey church.

" What is he doing that for ? " asked Norry.

" He is going to draw the church, and is looking to see which side he shall do first."

" Is that part of his lessons ? "

" No, he does it to please himself. He means to make two or three drawings of it to take home to his mamma."

" But this is not a pretty church. Why doesn't he do the one opposite our schoolroom ? She'd like that best."

" What, the cathedral ? O no, she wouldn't, Norry ! She used to come to this church Sunday after Sunday when she was a little girl, and that's why Robert is going to make her some drawings of it. Come with me, and I'll show you where she lived."

Mary led the way carefully between the graves, checking Norry whenever he showed an inclination to skip over one ; and opening a gate at the further end of the churchyard, she pointed to a small ivy-covered house a little distance off.

"We've had so many journeys to do that," said Mary, sighing, "and I don't think Robert is satisfied now."

"Who taught him to make pictures ?" asked Norry.

"His father. He was a great artist, and Robert hopes to be one too, some day, and earn money to keep his mother in a nice home again."

"But why doesn't she come back to this one ?"

"She can't, Norry ; her father is dead, and another clergyman is living here now."

They stood looking at the old church for a minute or two longer ; then Norry closed the gate, and they went back to their seat. Robert had settled himself down to his sketching by that time, and seemed to be working away very busily.

"Let us go and see what he's doing," said Norry.

"Not yet, we should only hinder him."

They sat still for some time longer ; but Norry, who was soon rested, would have been glad to run about again, and had a hard matter to keep himself quiet. However, he was so much impressed by the kindness of his new friends in bringing him, and the importance of the business on hand, that he felt bound to conduct himself discreetly. So by way of occupation of some kind, he tried to read the inscriptions on the nearest tombstones, but they were so effaced by time, that though he opened his eyes very wide one minute, or screwed them

up the next, as he had seen Dr. Hale do when looking at anything attentively, he could only make out
the capitals, and found it very dull work to guess at
what followed. At last Robert looked round, and
Mary seemed to take that as a signal that he did not
wish to be alone any longer, so she went over to him,
and sat down with Norry on the grass at his side.

" It's dull there, with nothing to amuse you, isn't it?"
said Robert. "Why didn't you bring your work ? "

" I had not time to get it to-day ; we came off in such
a hurry. How are you getting on ? "

" Not very well ; I think I could make a nicer sketch
from that bank in Mr. Elmer's garden. I'll begin there
to-morrow."

" And lose all your evening's work."

" Yes, I can't help that ; and besides, there's a whole
month before me yet."

" But you're forgetting Uncle Edward's prize, Robert."

" No I'm not ; I'll try for that too, but Arthur has
the best chance."

" Is that what you were both quarrelling about this
morning?"

" Yes ; Louis and I were translating the same page,
so we took turns in looking out the words, and then
Arthur said we were helping each other unfairly, and a
great many more disagreeable things."

" And then told papa you put yourself in a passion
with him. Why didn't you explain ? "

" Because what he said was partly true. I did feel
very angry, though I said nothing."

" But how could you help it ? Papa would not have

punished you if he had known how you had been pro-
voked."

"I don't think he would have considered that an
excuse, Mary; I shouldn't, if I had been judge. There,
now I'm ready."

The little folio was packed, and Robert tucked it under
his arm, and the three friends started homewards, passing through the vicarage garden on their way to see
how the church looked from the sloping lawn in front.

"She must have seen it oftenest from here," said
Mary, a remark that determined Robert at once to take
up his position on the lawn the next afternoon.

It was nearly dark when they reached home, and the
lamp was lit in Dr. Hale's study. Robert put away his
things quietly, and was leaving the room again when
Dr. Hale, who was writing at his own table, looked up
to ask if his lessons were ready for the next day.

"No, sir."

"Then suppose you come here and prepare them."

Robert gladly obeyed, and worked on diligently for
some time, with knit brow and compressed lips. When
giving his whole attention to anything he certainly was
not a pleasant-looking boy, and it was not surprising
that Norry had felt rather shy of making his acquaintance.

Soon after sunrise the next morning Robert was again
at work at Dr. Hale's table—a small steady one in the
pleasant bow-window, where there was plenty of light
for drawing, and before eight o'clock chimed from the
cathedral opposite, he had nearly completed his corrected
copy of the vicarage. Then the door opened gently,

and Mary Hale looked in to tell him breakfast was
ready.

"Has the post come in yet?" asked Robert.

"Yes; but there is no letter for you to-day."

He looked so disappointed that Mary tried to comfort him by saying that he was sure to get one on the
morrow.

"I hope so, but mamma is so punctual. She never
missed the day before."

"But you need not be uneasy about her. She said
she was better when she wrote last."

"She always says that," answered Robert sadly.

The sketches were put away, and then he and
Mary went into the dining-room, where the other members of the household were already gathered together
for family prayer. As they rose from their knees, Mrs.
Hale, a kind motherly woman, gave Robert a warmer
kiss than usual, for she was in all his secrets, and knew
how the non-arrival of the weekly letter from his mother
must be felt that morning.

As soon as lessons were over there was a grave dis-
cussion as to how the afternoon was to be spent.

"I think I shall go and sit in the Close," said Louis
Mead, "and see other folks work and play. It doesn't
seem like a half-holiday if you are doing anything
yourself."

"O Louis, how idle you are!" said Mary, reprov-
ingly.

"Well, what does it matter when work is done?
What's a half-holiday for, I should like to know, if it
isn't to give you a chance of enjoying yourself?"

"Which in your opinion means doing nothing," said Arthur Clayton. "Suppose you come and have a game of cricket with me."

"Too much trouble this hot day. Perhaps Robert will go with you."

"Oh, I didn't speak because I wanted any one. There'll be plenty of us without either of you; but he can go if he likes."

"I shan't have time," replied Robert.

"No, you'll be hard at work, I expect," said Arthur. "There'll be a fine chance of getting before us while we are having a little fun."

"I shall not be studying, Arthur, if you mean that."

"Perhaps you'll tell us what you are going to be about then."

"I think I can guess," said Louis; "looking after old Elmer's fruit. I saw him sitting on a gate staring at it the other day."

"He wasn't looking at the fruit," exclaimed Norry, indignantly.

"What was he doing then?"

"I think you'd better put away your books and slate, Norry," said Mary, "there'll be no time for clearing this afternoon."

There was a general rush to the littered table, for no one liked to lose a minute of the precious half-holiday. Books and papers were seized on by their different owners, and disposed of according to his or her particular way of clearing. Robert and Mary got through the business very creditably; Annie and Arthur with more regard to expedition than neatness; and Louis Mead limited his exertions to gathering his property into a heap before him, and indicating to Norry where it was to be put.

When dinner was over Norry ran panting back to the schoolroom, in great fear of being left behind; but, to his surprise, Robert seemed in no hurry to start.

" Ain't we going ? " he whispered at last to Mary.

" Not yet, you must wait a little."

It struck Norry that they wanted to see the other boys off first, so he stationed himself at the window, and watched the hall door with great attention. Presently he saw Arthur come out, and set off at full speed down the Close.

" There's one gone," he instantly announced.

" Which one ? " asked Mary.

Norry could not remember Arthur's name, so he designated him " the cricketing boy."

" Then we'll go," said Mary, and Robert got out his precious folio.

" But there's the other boy," said Norry.

" We don't mind him," answered Mary.

Norry was very glad to hear that, for, just then, the "other boy" strolled across the Close, and sat down on a shady bench in full view of the house; a position he was likely to occupy till the half-holiday was over. Mary ran to fetch her hat, and the next minute she and Norry were speeding along hand in hand after Robert, who had already started. As they turned the corner of the Close, Louis shouted to them from his bench, but Mary hurried on without answering, and, a little way down the lane, they saw Robert waiting for them.

" Is that a secret?" asked Norry, pointing to the folio under Robert's arm.

" No, not quite ; mamma and papa know about it, but we don't want Arthur to find it out, because he would tease Robert, and do all he could to hinder him."

" And is the other boy better natured ? "

" Yes ; and besides he would not take the trouble of interfering. Louis is a very idle boy."

" And a greedy one, too," said Norry. " He thought Robert wanted some old gentleman's fruit."

They had nearly overtaken Robert by that time, but, as he was in a hurry, he still kept on some paces in advance ; and, presently, Norry, who had been deep in thought on the subject, asked Mary why Arthur liked to tease Robert.

" I don't know. They never were very good friends, and now trying for the prize makes them worse."

" I suppose they both want to get it," said Norry, reflectively.

" Yes, and it makes a great many quarrels. Papa has been sorry Uncle Edward promised it, but it can't be helped now."

When the vicarage was reached, Robert spread out his folio, and went to work. Mary sat with her knitting a little apart from him, and told Norry he might look at the flowers and fruit if he thought he could do so without touching either. Norry declared himself quite equal to resisting any amount of temptation, so he was allowed to wander off wherever he pleased. Round the other side of the house he found more signs of life. A great dog was basking in the sun, and the sound of

women's voices came from one of the open windows.
Norry began to feel that he was trespassing dreadfully,
but the dog wagged his tail in such a friendly way, that
he ventured up to him, and stroked him gently.   Just
behind the dog, in a pleasant study, opening by a
French window on to the garden, was Mr. Elmer, a
kind-looking old gentleman, with white hair and bright
eyes, who startled Norry by suddenly calling out to
know who he was.

"Please, sir, I'm Norry Neal, from Dr. Hale's."

The answer seemed satisfactory.   Norry was invited
into Mr. Elmer's study, and next—rather an insult to
his seven years—lifted on to his knee ; but Mr. Elmer
looked so very old in the eyes of Master Norry, that
he submitted to the indignity with a tolerably good
grace.

"And have you come all this way to see me alone ?"
asked Mr. Elmer.

"No, sir ; I came with Robert and Mary."

"Oh, then, he's hard at work on our old church, I
suppose.   Dear me, I shouldn't have cared to spend
my half-holidays in such a way when I was a boy.
Wouldn't you like some fruit ?"

"No, sir, thank you ; Mary said I wasn't to have
any."

"Ah, because she is an honest little girl, and thought
she must take care of other people's property ; but you
need not be afraid to eat it if I give you permission.   Do
you think you could find a low doorway round at the
side of the house ?"

"Yes, sir ; I passed it just now."

"Then go and ask my housekeeper to give you a little basket."

Norry went on his errand very nimbly; and then he and Mr. Elmer wandered about among the fruit-trees, filling the basket with the ripest gooseberries they could find. When it could hold no more, Norry carried it in great exultation round to the two busy workers on the lawn. But there it was received with great indifference. Robert could not spare time to eat; and Mary said that, if Mr. Elmer did not mind lending them the basket, they had better take the fruit home.

Mr. Elmer made no objections, though he laughed at them for two steady old people. Then he sat down with Norry on a bench near, and talked about the school doings at Dr. Hale's till Mary remarked that it was time for them to be going home.

"And how have you got on?" asked Mr. Elmer, as Robert was putting up his sketch.

"I've done quite as much as I shall want, sir. The details can be put in at home from memory."

Mr. Elmer examined the sketch with great attention, and then told Robert he would make a first-rate artist some day.

"I hope so," Robert answered earnestly, for he was thinking of his mother.

They wished Mr. Elmer good evening, and then turned into the pleasant fields again, Norry carrying the little basket of fruit.

"We have not been to see Susan Turner lately," said Mary, as they entered the lane leading to the Close.

"No," answered Robert, glancing at the fruit; "suppose we go now."

"I think we should have time; tea is always a little later on half-holidays. Norry, do you care for your share of the gooseberries?"

Having picked them, and carried them so far, Norry did care very much, and was obliged to own it.

"Oh, never mind! we'll leave your share at the bottom of the basket. There'll be enough for Susan without."

Norry wondered who Susan Turner was, and felt rather ashamed of his own greediness; but he was a very little boy, and the gooseberries looked so ripe and luscious, that it was a hard matter to give them up.

They were entering the Close just then, and saw Louis Mead stretched on his bench exactly as they had left him.

"I don't think he has moved since we've been gone," said Norry.

"I dare say not," said Mary. "Don't let him see your basket, if you can help it, Norry."

They passed their own door, and then crossed the Close, Mary keeping Norry at her side, and dropping one end of her cape over his basket. But Louis, whose eyes were sharpened by their afternoon's exercise on the passers-by, spied it out, and shouted to them to tell him what was in it. They kept on without answering; but for once Louis could be quick in his movements, and he overtook them just as they were turning into one of the quiet streets leading out of the Close.

"Keep away!" screamed Norry, as Louis clutched unceremoniously at the basket. "It's not for you."

"Oh, isn't it? Come, we'll soon see; I mean to have my share."

"No, we can't spare you any," said Mary; "we're carrying it to a poor sick girl."

"Oh, that's a likely story!" and Louis made another dash at the basket, and sent some of the gooseberries rolling on the pavement. Robert seized him, and held him firmly back, notwithstanding his kicks and struggles to get free.

"You had better go on without me, Mary," said Robert.

Mary took Norry's hand, and the two ran together down the street.

"He is a very bad boy!" said Norry, when breathlessness obliged them to slacken their pace a little.

"No, he is not, Norry—only a greedy one."

Not feeling his own conscience quite clear on the score of greediness, Norry was silent for a minute; then he remarked,—

"But he is an idle one too; you said so this afternoon."

"Yes; but I did not say he was bad. When I was ill last summer, he sat and read to me quite as often as the others did; and once he brought me some jam that I know he wanted himself. So you see he can be kind and unselfish sometimes."

But this statement did not quite mollify Norry's indignant feelings, and he rather comforted himself with the hope that Dr. Hale had seen Louis's misconduct from the window, and would give him a long lesson for it.

They soon turned out of the broad quiet street, and Norry got bewildered in a multitude of steep narrow ways, where the houses were very small, and, in his eyes, very disagreeable.

"Does Susan live here?" he asked, as they stopped before an open door.

Mary answered "Yes," and led the way through a dark passage, stopping at the foot of a staircase that seemed darker still, to take the basket of fruit from Norry—a wise precaution, as he stumbled more than once in toiling up the steep ascent; and half the gooseberries, had they been in his charge, would, no doubt, have rolled to the bottom.

A very weak voice said, "Come in," in answer to Mary's low tap at one of the doors on the dingy landing, and they went into a small room, close and miserable from neglect and poverty, where a little girl, of about the same age as Mary, was lying in bed. Norry hoped that the gooseberries would be put down somewhere directly, and that they should run away again, but Mary went round to the bedside to kiss the poor sick girl, and say she hoped she was better.

"Just the same," was the quiet answer. "Thank you for coming."

"Have you been alone long?"

"Yes; all day. Mother went out early, and father—" Susan paused, and Mary looked down so pityingly at her, that Norry thought there must be something about father to be sorry for.

"I have brought you some nice fresh fruit," said Mary. "Can I find anything to put it in ?"

Susan thanked her, and pointed to a small corner cupboard. Mary went to it, and turned over the contents of the lower shelf—a few pieces of crockery that had been thrust in unwashed after breakfast that morning. One clean plate, that had evidently escaped use from its unserviceable condition, was found, at last, and laid beside the basket of fruit.

"I am afraid it won't hold them," said Mary, finding the gooseberries had an obstinate tendency to roll out of the plate by its broken corner. "I'll see if I can wash another."

"Couldn't you leave the basket?" asked Susan. "It looks so pretty ; and Tom shall bring it round to you in the morning."

"No, I'm afraid I can't," said Mary, "for some of it has to go back with us."

"No, I don't want any," said Norry, "I'd rather she had it all."

"Then I'll leave the basket. And never mind about sending it, Susan ; some one shall come for it."

Mary said good-bye to Susan ; then she and Norry went down-stairs into the sweet, fresh summer air again.

"I'm so glad I gave up my share," said Norry, who felt that he had made a great sacrifice. "She wants it more than I do."

"Yes ; we can give up a great deal when we know that other people want it. That is why papa says we ought to visit the sick and poor, or else we forget them."

"And do you go about these nasty streets finding them out?"

"No, papa does that; and then he tells us of some one we may visit, and carry nice things to, as we can spare them."

"There's a piece of cake still left that I brought from home," said Norry. "I should like her to have that. Do you think we may go and see her again to-morrow?"

"I don't know; but I dare say one of the boys will fetch the basket in the morning, so you can send your cake then."

Finding, on reaching home, that tea was not quite ready, they went into the schoolroom to put out a few lessons that would have to be studied that evening. Only Louis was there, bending a very sulky face over a book.

"See what you've got me into," he growled, without looking up. "Here's a long piece!"

Norry thought Mary would instantly tell him that he had his own greediness to thank for it; but she answered gently,

"I am very sorry, Louis, but you know we did not mean it."

"Well, never mind; I'll have it all out with him before long."

"Do you mean with Robert?"

"Yes; what business had he to interfere?"

"He was quite right, Louis; you know that, and will soon own it too, I'm sure."

Very much to Norry's surprise Louis did own it

directly after that punishment lesson was said.   He went into the bow-window, where Mary was sitting with her work, and telling her that he was very sorry for his ill-behaviour, promised better things for the future.

"Perhaps it would not have happened if you had not been so idle all the afternoon," said Mary.   "I think we ought to do something even on our half-holidays."

"Do you?   Well, I'll see next time; only it seems rather hard."

"Oh no, it does not, when you once try."

Louis went back to his place, and prepared his lessons for the next day.   As he was putting them away, Mary said,

"Would you mind going to Church Row in the morning to fetch a basket I left there?"

"How can I, when I've got to set to work directly after breakfast?"

"But you can go before; there'll be plenty of time."

"O yes, for you; you get up so early."

"And so can you for once.   I'll wake you."

"So you are going to be taken in hand," said Arthur; "I hope it will do you good."

"I don't mind if it does," returned Louis, good-humouredly.

And very early next morning Mary was at Norry's bedside, asking him for the piece of cake he was going to send to Susan Turner.   He sat up, and stared at her without speaking, feeling either a little sleepy and dull of comprehension, or loth to part with his small store.

"Don't send it unless you like, Norry."

"O yes, I don't mind. Only will it be safe if Louis takes it? Won't he eat it?"

"No, I think he is to be trusted now. Where shall I find it?"

Having hidden it in some out-of-the-way corner, Norry thought it would be best to hunt it out himself, which he did; and then Mary wrapped it up neatly, and carried it down to Louis.

They were all in the breakfast-room when Louis came panting in with the basket in his hand. Everybody looked up in surprise, except the two who were in the secret of his morning's expedition, and Dr. Hale asked him where he had been. He had just finished his explanation when the servants came in, bringing the letters, which had arrived later than usual that morning. Robert glanced anxiously at them as they passed him, but they were thrown down on the table in a confused heap, and he had to wait patiently till prayers were over before they were given to their owners. Then Mrs. Hale put one into his hand, and told him she would excuse him if he liked to open it in the school-room. Robert thanked her, seized his letter, and hurried away. He was so long gone that breakfast was nearly over before he came back, and took his place at Mary's side. Mrs. Hale passed him a cup of tea; but both that and his plate of bread-and-butter were nearly untouched when the others got up from table.

"Stop a minute," said Mrs. Hale, as Robert was rising too.   "You have not finished your breakfast."

Robert sat down again, and as soon as they were alone, Mrs. Hale went round to him, and asked him, with her kind hand on his shoulder, if he had any bad news.   Robert gave her the letter, then hid away his face, and tried to check his deep sobs while she read it. It was very short, and penned in a faint, tremulous hand.

"I don't see anything there to alarm you, Robert," said Mrs. Hale.

"Haven't you noticed the writing?"

"It is unsteady.   But you know your mother is not strong."

"And was too ill to write yesterday."

"She does not say so."

"No, but she would not have let anything else prevent her."

Mrs. Hale knew even more about Mrs. Warner's illness than Robert did, and felt she could not speak of it very hopefully.   There was but one way to comfort him.

"Robert," she said softly, "you know in whose hands your mother is?"

"Yes, ma'am."

"Then you must trust Him fully.   If you had some tender pet—a little bird, perhaps—would you be afraid to leave it in my charge?"

"No, I should know it was quite safe.   Oh, it isn't that!"

"What is it, then?"

Robert did not answer; and at last Mrs. Hale said—

"Isn't it that you don't like her to be in any one's hands but yours?"

"Yes, ma'am, perhaps so. But you know what I have been looking forward to so long—to be with her, and work for her."

"Yes, I know, Robert." A kind, unselfish wish, which Mrs. Hale loved him all the better for cherishing so deeply, but which she feared would never be gratified.

A little later Robert went to his work in the study, and tried to conceal his trouble by extra diligence. So he kept on day after day, and Dr. Hale, noticing his grave face and sunken eyes, sometimes told him that the prize was not worth all that earnest striving for. Only Mrs. Hale and Mary knew that he had almost forgotten it, and that all he really cared to take home at the holidays were the drawings. On those he spent all his spare time, going to Nunstead whenever he could get away for an hour or two; and often, in his anxiety to make his sketches faithful copies of his mother's early home, lingering in the old churchyard or vicarage garden to do his task again. Arthur Clayton watched his diligence with very unfriendly eyes. He knew nothing of the visits to Nunstead, but thought, like Dr. Hale, that he was only trying hard to get the prize. This conclusion only made him more eager to win it himself. He had no idea, as he said, of any one getting before him, and it was a rule with Arthur, whenever he could not succeed in attaining what he aimed at himself, to use every means—often unfair ones—to prevent others being more successful. Once when he and Robert were striving to see which should first reach the topmost branch of a tree, and Robert's hand was stretched out to grasp it, Arthur gave him a blow that sent him crashing down through the green boughs to the ground. It was a cowardly action, and Robert rose with a white face and fixed lips. But he was not hurt; and both Mary and Louis, who had pressed up to ask him, shrunk back in affright, as they met his gleaming eyes. Arthur too slunk away, and from that time it had been whispered about among the children, till it got to Dr. and Mrs. Hale's ears that Robert had a fearful temper. Many a punishment lesson had his evil repute won for him. Arthur's usual explanation of any dispute between himself and Robert was, "Oh, he's always getting into such awful passions!" and this statement having been frequently repeated, Dr. Hale spoke seriously to Robert, one afternoon, in the schoolroom, on the evils of unrestrained temper, comparing a passionate man to the owner of a savage dog, ready to bite every one near him.

"But would the man be much to blame, papa, for having such a dog if he kept him in, and tried to tame him?" asked Mary.

"No, certainly not," answered Dr. Hale. "But Robert does not seem to be doing so with his temper." And Mary said no more, as it was evident that everybody thought her remark had nothing to do with the case in hand.

When the last fortnight's work was entered on,

Arthur began to see that he did not stand so well in
his studies as Robert ; and that, if matters went on so,
he should certainly lose the prize. Something must be
done ; but it never occurred to Arthur that that "something" had better be a little extra diligence on his own
part. He could not rise early in the morning, as Robert
did, nor give up his half-holiday. Both sacrifices in-
volved far too much self-denial, so they were not even
attempted. His only plan was to throw impediments
in his rival's path ; an easier way, he thought, of keeping up with him than running faster himself. But
it surprised him a good deal to see how patiently the
hindrances were taken ; how quietly Robert bore the
loss of his own books, and waited till Arthur or Louis
could spare theirs ; and how little he seemed to care
about the disappearance from his slate of sums or exercises that had been carefully prepared. Annie Hale
and Norry often laughed, and said the fairies had to do
with his things, but Robert knew whom he had to thank
for all the unkind tricks that were played him. Sometimes, seeing his utter indifference to the worst he could
do, Arthur began to fancy Robert did not really care for
the prize. But then, if not, why did he give up his
half-holidays, and long pleasant summer evenings? It
was very puzzling ; and Arthur watched him more
narrowly than ever, but was none the wiser. That
Robert was really working very hard was all he could
see. There was always a book or writing folio under
his arm whenever he went out ; and, if he happened
to be broken in on unexpectedly, he was sure to be
found bending over something that was instantly hur-

ried out of sight. What was it? Some private notes to help his memory? And, in order to answer the question satisfactorily, Arthur took the first opportunity that presented itself of prying into Robert's desk. But he found very little there except a packet of letters neatly tied up, and some delicate drawings; things that he threw contemptuously back, wondering how Robert could trouble himself to keep such rubbish.

"You'd better give up," said Louis, one half-holiday that he was enjoying after his own fashion. "Robert is sure to win."

"Is he? How do you know that?"

"Why, don't you see how he's working?"

"Yes; but what's that got to do with it?"

"Why, everything, I should think. If not, there might be a chance for me."

"Well, perhaps there is; just as good a one, at all events, as for him. It's a pity he takes so much trouble for nothing."

Louis laughed, and stretched himself out more at his ease on the two chairs he was occupying. He knew that Arthur's boastful tone was only assumed, and that he was really in great fear of Robert's outstripping him. But Norry, who was standing by listening, not being quite so clearsighted, felt very wrathful, and eager to say something in defence of his friend's dignity.

"He doesn't seem very sure about the prize himself," continued Arthur, "or he would not look so solemn."

"Perhaps he's something else to trouble him," said Louis.

" Yes, it's sitting in that grave-garden so much," said
Norry, who had found the long hours in the Nunstead
churchyard rather trying to his own patience sometimes;
" that's what it is."

" Hey, what do you mean?" asked Arthur.

But Norry felt he had already said too much, and did
not answer.

" Come, you'd better speak out, or I'll make you!"

" No, you won't," replied Norry, " not if you kill
me."

" Oh, what, it's a secret, is it—and you're in it?"

" Well, why shouldn't I be?"

" Oh, I don't know, I've not the least objection.
Only all you've got to do now is to let me into it."

" Then I'm not going to do it."

" Let him alone, can't you?" said Louis. " He means
old Elmer's churchyard. I know Robert goes there
sometimes."

" But that's more than a mile off. He could find
plenty of quiet corners to work in nearer home."

" But he mightn't like them so well. Don't you
know his mother was brought up at the vicarage."

Arthur replied that he had heard something about it;
but his own mind not being burdened with any tender
associations, he asked Louis with a stare what that had
to do with it.

" Oh, you'd better ask him if you want to know,"
replied Louis, lazily. " Here, Norry, there's a man
crossing the road with cherries. Just go and buy me
a penn'orth, will you?"

Norry ran out on his errand very willingly. When

he came back Arthur was gone, so he sat down with
Louis, and got a very fair share of the cherries. Soon
after they were eaten, and the stones cracked—a business which, being left entirely to Norry, was not very
speedily accomplished—Arthur came in with a careless
air, and slow step. But there was a crimson glow in
his face that made Norry suspect he had not taken
things quite so quietly while he was away. He threw
himself down at the other end of the room, and presently asked Louis with a yawn, what he had told him
about that old place, Nunstead Vicarage.

" Nothing particular that I know of. What do you
want to hear about it ? "

" Anything you've got to tell me."

" Well, that won't be much.—I say, Norry, that man
isn't gone yet. Can you lend me a penny ? "

" No," answered Norry.

" Oh, then, there won't be any more cherries to-
day ! " and Louis sank back with a groan.

" Yes, there will," said Arthur, " as many as you
like ! Here's a shilling, Norry ; you may spend it all,
and we'll have a feast."

" No, we won't," said Louis. " Norry, you give him
his money back."

" What for—what do you mean ? " asked Arthur.

" That I'm not going to be bought over by a penn'orth
of cherries."

" Who talks of buying you over ? What a fool you
are ! "

" That's likely enough," answered Louis, with supreme
indifference.

" Then you don't mean to have the cherries ? "

The tempting basket was, just then, being carried past the window, so Louis prudently drew back a little, and then answered steadily,

" No, you may eat 'em yourself."

" I suppose they've given you more on the other side to keep the secret," sneered Arthur.

" What secret ? "

" Why, Robert's. But if I want to find it out, I can do so without your help."

" Very well, try."

" Perhaps I know it already. I could tell you where he is, and what he's doing."

" Because you've been to see. I thought so when you came in."

" Did you ? If you're so sharp, it's a pity you can't see your own interest better than to fight his battles. You know he despises you ; and it was only the other day he brought you in looking like a whipped dog."

" Served me right And he'll do it the next time he catches me behaving like a brute, I dare say."

Arthur felt very angry ; however, he kept his wrath to himself, knowing by experience that its exhibition would not interfere in the least with Louis's serene enjoyment of his half-holiday. He had, as Louis suspected, been to Nunstead, seen Robert putting the finishing touches to his last sketch, and ran home, greatly wondering what he was taking so much trouble for. Self-interest being, in Arthur's estimation, the only motive likely to prompt any one to exertion, he came to the conclusion, at last, that Robert was selling his drawings for pocket-money ; and this surmise was presently announced to Louis, with extreme satisfaction at its remarkable sagacity.

" Perhaps he does," was Louis's answer.

" And lets you share the profits ? "

" No, there you're wrong," replied Louis, rummaging in his empty pockets. " I only wish he did, I should have a fine time of it ! "

" He doesn't sell his drawings," said Norry, indignantly. " They're for his mother. He is saving them all up for her."

" That's a likely story," said Arthur.

" What, that a·boy should love his mother !" said Louis. " Yes ; I suspect that's beyond you, sharp as you are. Come, you'd better give it up ! "

Arthur began to think he had, for the time, at least, so he took up his hat and strolled out again.

Presently Robert came in, looking tired and worn ; and as he put away his folio, Norry told him, in great excitement, that Arthur had been all the way to Nunstead to find out his secret.

" Who told him I was gone there ? " asked Robert.

" I did," replied Louis, expecting to be collared and shaken the next minute. But Robert only answered quietly that it did not matter, as his work was quite done there now, and he should not have to go any more.

" Oh, very well. Only if you have any secret, I'd advise you to look after it."

" But I haven't one ; at least I don't want to keep it any longer. Would you like to see what I've done ?"

Louis lounged round to the back of Robert's chair, and stood there while he spread out his drawings. There were three views of Nunstead Vicarage and three of the church.

"What did you do so many for?" he asked.

"Because I hardly liked to leave any part out. This view of the house is from the church porch, and I almost think mamma will like it the best of all."

"It's a nice drawing. How hard you must have worked to get them done!"

"Yes, I have; and other things have been neglected. But I can make up for lost time now."

"Do you mean that you've cared more about finishing these drawings than getting the prize?"

"Yes, a great deal. And if I thought I could improve them by copying them again, I'd set about it the first thing to-morrow morning. Mamma will care more for these pictures than the prize."

"Well, she's worth taking a little trouble for," said Louis thoughtfully; "there are not many like her."

"How do you know? You have never seen her."

"Yes, I have. Don't you remember me being sent home after the fever?"

"Yes; when mamma came to nurse me. But you had gone before she arrived."

"But I met her at one of the stations on the road. She came into a room where I was stretched out, feeling thoroughly done up,—for I'd hardly got over my illness,—and she made a soft pillow for me with her shawl, and talked so pleasantly, that I was quite sorry when our man came to tell me the next train was up."

"But how do you know the lady was my mother?"

"Because she put her name and address in a little book she gave me just as she was bidding me good-bye. She told me I was to write to her."

"And you never did?"

"No, what was the good? But I've often thought of her, and read her book. You shall see it if you like."

He ran off to fetch it, and nearly fell over Arthur Clayton in the doorway.

"Halloa!" said Louis, "what are you hiding there for?"

"Hiding! what do you mean? I've as much right to go in at a door as you have to come out of it, I suppose?"

Louis shrugged his shoulders and hurried up-stairs Just as he had found his book, the bell rang for tea, so he thrust the little volume into his pocket and went down to the dining-room. As soon as tea was over, the pupils reassembled round the study table to prepare their lessons for the next day, a work that always took some time; and the evening was far advanced before Robert and Louis could betake themselves to a quiet corner, and turn over the pages of Mrs. Warner's little book together. Dr. Hale, who had remained behind in the study with Mary and Norry, went into the drawing-room in search of his wife, but finding she had gone out, he returned to his pleasant seat in the bow-window, and told Mary, who was still busy clearing, to fetch her needlework and sit with him. Norry, who was specially privileged as the youngest of the party, drew in his stool too, and the three settled down very cosily together. Before long it began to grow dark, so work was put aside, and they looked out into the Close, where a party of boys were playing, Robert and Louis among the number.

" I'm glad to see they are getting more sociable," said Dr. Hale. " It has been quite a trouble to me to have my boys constantly quarrelling."

" I think Louis is trying to behave better," said Norry, with the gravity of threescore.

" Yes, papa, to be one of your heroes," said Mary.

" What do you mean ?" asked Dr. Hale.

" Don't you remember saying once, that to struggle with our faults was a battle worth fighting, papa ?"

" Yes ; we were talking of temper—of Robert's, I think. I wish I could see him trying to overcome his."

Just then Mrs. Hale looked in, and called Norry, telling him it was time to go to bed.

" Must he come directly ?" asked Dr. Hale. " We are making ourselves so very comfortable here."

" Oh ! are you there ?" and Mrs. Hale advanced into the room ; " I did not see you."

It was nearly dark, and the bow-window in which Dr. Hale was sitting was a very old-fashioned one, deeply arched out on either side beyond the frame, so that, as he leaned back in his easy chair, his figure, which was quite hidden in front by an ample muslin curtain, could not be outlined against the faint light outside.

" I suppose it is time to call the boys in," said Dr. Hale.

"Not quite. I told Robert he might have another half-hour as I passed him, just now. Poor boy; he seemed to be enjoying himself so much."

"Shall you tell him to-night?" asked Dr. Hale.

"Yes; it would not be right to keep it from him any longer. Besides, she wishes him to know now."

"Isn't his mamma so well?" asked Mary.

"No, dear, she is very ill."

Mary's tears began to fall quickly, but silently. She had seen something of Mrs. Warner, and loved her fondly; but, just then, she was thinking of all poor Robert's plans, and the bitter disappointment there was before him.

"I think I shall tell him when he is in his own room to-night," said Mrs. Hale.

"He will want to go home at once, no doubt," remarked the doctor.

"Yes, and that will be best. John, I've been thinking I ought to go with him; but I don't know that I can be spared."

"Hardly, Mary. We shall find it a difficult matter to get on without you; but we mustn't think of that if you wish to go. He'll want some one to help and comfort him, poor boy! We shall break up in little more than a week, and then, if you are still away, I can fetch you."

There was a minute's silence; then Mrs. Hale told Norry he must go, and led him away, saying to her husband, as she left the room, that she should soon be back again. Mary followed to see if she could do anything to help her mamma, and Dr. Hale was left alone. It was his usual time for enjoying an hour's quiet reading, but his mind was full of Robert's trouble then, and the painful journey before his wife; so he sat still thinking of both.

Presently the door opened, and somebody moved about the room. It was one of the boys, Dr. Hale knew, and he took no further notice. The recollection that he was himself quite hidden from sight did not occur to him. A key was turned sharply in a lock, and the rustling of paper followed. Then two other boys burst into the hall, and one of them came across into the study.

" Halloa !" said the last comer, who was Robert, " is that you, Arthur ?"

" Yes; I'm hunting for my—my atlas, but I can't find it anywhere."

" Never mind ; I'll give you mine."

" But I would rather have my own. Will you light the lamp ?"

" No ; I don't think Dr. Hale would like it."

" What nonsense ! Well, here's a taper ; it won't frighten you to see that burning, I suppose. And here's some matches."

Robert lit one, but it burnt dimly, and Arthur said he would find some paper."

" But I don't want any," said Robert.

" Yes, you do. Here's a bit ; no, that isn't large enough ; here's another.

Arthur was tearing up a great deal of paper unnecessarily ; but as nothing more important than old exercises was ever left on that table, there seemed no fear of his doing any mischief.

The taper was lit, and Dr. Hale was just going to step out from his quiet corner, when a sudden exclamation from Robert—one of mingled pain and passion —made him draw back again, and look silently on. Through the muslin curtains he could see quite well all that was passing in the room.

Robert was standing just opposite, with a white, fixed face, and on the table, beside his open desk, were his drawings, torn and crumpled. For a moment he seemed half stunned ; then he turned, with a clenched fist, upon Arthur, who slunk back, and got the table between himself and Robert. But the next instant the raised arm fell again, and the look of passion faded from Robert's face.

"Well," said Arthur, who seemed considerably reassured by the change ; "what do you mean by staring like that ?"

"O Arthur ! you don't know what you have done !"

The words were spoken very faintly, and with more than one deep gasp for breath.

"Yes, I do—torn up some of your scraps ; you should not have left them about."

"I did not. You must have taken them out of my desk on purpose to destroy them."

"It's a story ! a base, shameful story !" and Arthur sprang upon Robert, and struck him with all his force upon the forehead. He received the blow unflinchingly, only tightening the pressure of the clenched hand against his side. It seemed hard work to keep it there.

"Now then, you may go with your story to Dr. Hale, if you like, and see if he believes you."

Arthur had no opportunity for any further display of prowess, for his collar was firmly grasped by Dr. Hale, whose fingers tingled to shake him well ; but he did not like to show less self-control than his own pupil had just done ; so he told him quietly to go into the dining-room, and wait there till he could speak to him. Then, after Arthur had slunk away, Dr. Hale laid his hand on Robert's shoulder, and said he was very sorry for what had happened.

"Thank you, sir ; but I think I shall have time to do them again ; it will only be the loss of the prize."

"And I suppose that was Arthur's purpose in destroying them."

"I cannot help thinking so, sir ; but it may have been an accident."

But Dr. Hale had no doubt on the subject. He had heard the stealthy feet about the room, and the sharp click of the key in the lock ; however, those were facts to be discussed between himself and Arthur alone, so he said nothing about them.

"What made you lay such a restraint on your temper just now, my boy ?" he asked.

"I promised my mother that I would, sir."

"And had you no other reason ? "

"Yes, sir. Our Lord has said, 'Blessed are the meek.'"

"And you would like to be of their number ? I think you will, my boy, but it's a hard fight for you."

They turned to look at the damage the drawings had

Page 44.

sustained, and it was found that only two had escaped. The others were torn in several places.

"I have the pencil sketches by me still, sir," said Robert, "so that I can copy them again."

"Not yet," said Dr. Hale, gravely ; "you must let them be for a while."

He thought it was a good time then to tell him about his mother's illness, but did not quite know how to do it. With either of the other boys he would not have felt the same difficulty. But Robert was quick of comprehension, and read the meaning of Dr. Hale's sad, perplexed face at a glance.

"My mother is not so well ?" he said.

"No, my boy," was all Dr. Hale could answer.

"Have you known it long, sir ?"

"Yes—at least, for some weeks."

"And not told me !"

"It was her wish. She trusted that a great grief would have been spared to you."

"And is there no hope now, sir ? "

"I wouldn't say that, but I fear not."

Robert sat quite still for some minutes, with his face in his hands. Then he rose, and asked if he might go. Dr. Hale wished him good-night, and as he saw his colourless, grief-stricken face go past him, he felt sorry he had not left to his wife the telling of the sad news. She came in just as Robert was leaving the room, and he stopped for a moment to say "good-night," as he passed out.

"Poor boy ! you have told him," said Mrs. Hale, as soon as Robert was gone.

"Yes, and I am sorry for it now. You would have done it better."

"No, I shouldn't. I don't think it would matter much how he was told ; he would think only of her."

"Well, perhaps so. He is so different to our other boys—has stronger feelings and passions, but both under right control. He will have a great deal to suffer, I am afraid, as he goes through the world."

The little taper was flickering out, so Dr. Hale lit the lamp and told his wife all that had just passed, recollecting, as he came to the end of his account, that Arthur was waiting for him in the dining-room.

"And how will you deal with him?" asked Mrs. Hale, sadly, for Arthur's case seemed even a more sorrowful one than Robert's.

"I hardly know. At all events I can't see him to-night, I must wait till I'm cool." And he sent a servant to tell Arthur he was to go to bed directly.

Then he sat for a little while longer with Mrs. Hale, talking of her journey the next day, and discussing plans for the comfort of the poor sick lady.

"I should like to stay and nurse her," said Mrs. Hale, "only she must look on me as such a stranger."

"But she won't after you have been with her half an hour. Act as you think best when you get there."

"And then there's home."

"With Mary, a most trustworthy little housekeeper, to see after it. If Mrs. Warner were rich, I should say, come back by the next train ; but as it is, I think there are many reasons for your staying a little while to see how matters are going on."

" I have sometimes feared she has been making great sacrifices to keep Robert here," said Mrs. Hale.

" It is very likely. There is a deep affection between them, and they are both capable of any amount of self-devotion. If the worst should come, as we fear," continued Dr. Hale, after a short silence, " tell her Robert will come back to us as our son."

" Yes, it will be a comfort to her to know that."

A little later Mrs. Hale went up to Robert's room, thinking it would lighten his sorrow to know that he would see his mother the next day. She left her light outside, and went softly in, asking him if he was in bed.

" No, ma'am, not yet."

He was lying on the floor, as quiet and motionless as if he had been asleep. Mrs. Hale sat down beside him, and pillowed his head tenderly on her lap. He scarcely seemed to notice her, but after some time she felt his tears on her hand, and knew then that he could bear to speak of his trouble.

" I have come to tell you that you will see her to-morrow, Robert ; we are going together."

" Thank you. I ought to have been with her long ago. Why has it been kept from me ? What is it ? "

" Something that has caused her much suffering, Robert, and that we thought the doctor's skill could have removed, but—"

" Yes, I know. Don't tell me *that*, I can't bear to hear it again to-night."

It was distressing to hear his deep quiet sobs ; but

Mrs. Hale knew that it was best to let his grief take its own course for a while.

"If she could only have had a few happy years first," he said, "I should not have minded so much.   But her life has been so hard !"

"Yes, I know, my boy ; and you meant to make it bright for her.   So we plan sometimes for our best friends, and then we have to learn in sorrow the precious truth that God has provided 'some better thing' for them."

Then Mrs. Hale told him of some bereavement that had come to her very early in life.   He did not pay much attention, but the low tones of her voice soothed him ; and when she had finished, and told him he must go to bed to get strength for the next day's journey, he rose directly, and said he was ready.

Mrs. Hale stole back into his room more than once that night, and each time found him quite still in bed, but she could hardly hope that he was sleeping.

They started on their journey very early the next day.   Dr. Hale went with them to the train, and on his return summoned Arthur into the study.   They had not met at breakfast that morning, Arthur having chosen to keep in his room ; and at the first glance at his haggard face, Dr. Hale saw he must have passed a wretched night.   He held his head, however, even higher than ever.

"I wish to leave, sir !" was his passionate interruption of Dr. Hale's first words.

"I am not surprised at that, Arthur."

"Why, sir?"

" Because you feel that you have forfeited our respect, and I am afraid that you are not disposed to win it back in the right way."

" I am not going to do anything mean, sir."

" Your idea of what is mean, and mine, are very different, Arthur. We found that out some time ago. In my opinion nothing could be meaner than your conduct last night."

" What, in tearing up a few trumpery drawings, sir ? "

" Yes, when you knew that their destruction would give pain to their owner. But that is not all. How did you get possession of those drawings ? "

Arthur was silent, and Dr. Hale went on—

" By creeping into a room in the dark, unlocking a desk, and stealing the contents."

" Stealing, sir ! "

" Yes; I think that is the term you would apply to such an action had you seen it performed by one of the servants. And now I have sent for you to ask if you have any apology to offer ? "

" No, sir, I wish to leave ! "

" You think that the easiest way of getting over your difficulty."

" It is the most gentlemanly one, sir."

" Such a term as that cannot apply to anything connected with your share in last night's business, Arthur. It was base and cowardly from beginning to end, and you know that, though you try to brave it out."

Arthur coloured, and his bright blue eyes wavered a little in their fixed stare on Dr. Hale's face, but the next minute he had resumed his defiant attitude.

D

"I am sorry for you," said Dr. Hale. "I should have been glad to do you good, and see you go out into the world prepared to do your work in a brave upright spirit, but if you are determined to take your own way you must do so. I will write to your mother some time to-day."

"I have already done so, sir."

"And told her all the circumstances?"

"Yes, as I see them, sir. And she will not put the same construction on them that you do."

This was a statement Dr. Hale could not contradict, for he knew that Mrs. Clayton was always blind to her son's faults.

"Well, it matters little to me what you may induce others to think of your conduct, Arthur," he said; "your own conscience condemns you, and you cannot doubt what is the judgment of One who is greater than your conscience and knoweth all things."

Arthur was silent for a moment, but the evil spirit of pride which he had so long cherished in his bosom stifled the feeling of penitence which this solemn appeal had awakened, and his only reply was,

"Then you have no objection to my leaving, sir?"

"Certainly not. A boy who will not make any effort to govern his bad passions is no fit associate for my own children."

Arthur left the room not a little surprised and humbled. He belonged to one of the best county families, and expected that Dr. Hale would have been glad to keep him on any terms. So he still hoped, until, some time the next day, he saw his mother's carriage outside, and found he was really to go back in it.

A few days after the Midsummer holidays were over Robert came back to Dr. Hale's, now his only home. The children were in the hall to receive him, and Mary held Norry back with womanly gravity when he seemed likely to launch into too lively a demonstration of pleasure at the sight of his old friend.

"Hush, Norry, you forget!"

She was thinking of the great sorrow that had passed into Robert's life while he was away. Norry was instantly sobered into more discreet behaviour, and looked quietly on as Robert followed Mrs. Hale into the dining-room without stopping to bestow a smile of recognition on any one.

"He'll come to us presently," said Mary; "mamma will know best how to comfort him now."

They went into the study, Louis and Annie following, and sat down in the bow-window to talk over all the little plans they had been forming for some days past to make Robert's new home pleasant to him. He had come back to warm, generous hearts, ready to sacrifice their best things in his service. Even in his grief he had a grateful consciousness of that, and his was not a nature likely to forget such kindness in after life.

LENA'S OFFERING.

" A gift is as a precious stone in the eyes of him that hath it ; whithersoever it turneth, it prospereth."—PROV. xvii. 8.

A GROUP of children were standing round one of the upper windows of a house in Harley Street, eagerly watching the arrival of visitors below. Carriage after carriage put down its gaily-dressed occupants, and then rolled slowly away. Gradually the hot dusty street began to darken, and the bustle subsided. One by one the children quitted their station, and at last only a boy of ten or twelve still lingered at the window. Before long his patience was rewarded : a cab heavily laden with luggage drew up at the door. There was, of course, a general rush to the window again, and eager eyes peered curiously out.

"I expect it's old Mosely by the style," remarked the persevering watcher.

"And brought his boxes with him, Tom," said Frank, his elder brother ; "that's a likely affair !"

This idea caused a good deal of amusement, in the midst of which one of the children suddenly discovered that there was a little girl in the cab.

"So there is," said Frank. "Why, I shouldn't wonder if it were Lena Halcot ! Is she expected to-day, Miss Emerson ?"

Miss Emerson, their teacher, an elderly lady, who was trying, somewhere in the background, to rest a weary pair of eyes, replied that she had not heard anything about it, and sighed heavily over the prospect of soon having an addition to the noisy little party already under her charge.

"Is the little girl alone?" she asked.

"No, there's a gentleman with her; mamma said she was coming home under the charge of a clergyman, so it must be Lena."

A few minutes after, Miss Emerson was summoned from the room; and the next the children heard was that the gentleman and the little girl were taking tea in the library.

"Then it is Lena!" said Frank; "so I shall go and see what she is like."

"Mamma said we were not to go down," said Grace, the only daughter of the family; "and Miss Emerson will be cross if you do, Frank."

"Who cares for Miss Emerson?" said Frank, and he strode off with the dignity of a young gentleman but lately emancipated from governess thraldom.

On his return he was eagerly questioned—"Is it Lena, Frank? How old is she? Do you like her?"

"No, I do not," was his answer to the last question; "she's a stumpy disagreeable-looking little thing, and will be a regular nuisance, you'll see."

This prediction being received as likely to be fulfilled, was, as might be expected, speedily verified. Lena had scarcely been a week among her new friends, before it was unanimously affirmed that she was in everybody's way. Her chief fault seemed to be moping, a habit likely to be indulged in by a quiet child thrown suddenly among strangers, but which no one seemed disposed to regard charitably. The poor child herself was, of course, the greatest sufferer from her inability to settle down contentedly with her aunt and cousins. She was an orphan, both parents having died some months previously, under very sad circumstances, at a distant station in India. Her aunt, Mrs. Jenyon, in her first grief for the loss of her brother, from whom she had been estranged for many years, in consequence of her dislike to his wife, kindly offered to take charge of their only remaining child. So Lena came, but for some months passed a dull listless life in the midst of her merry cousins. With Miss Emerson she was always in disgrace, from her unwillingness or inability to do the tasks that were set her; and yet dreary as the hours of study seemed, they were, perhaps, the pleasantest portion of her day. As soon as they were over, Lena's first care was to escape from the wild spirits and teasing ways of her cousins, by taking refuge in some quiet hiding-place—a habit that had made Master Frank, who was going through a course of Natural History with his tutor, declare that she belonged to the order cheiroptera, and that he intended to get up some night on purpose to have the pleasure of seeing her frisk about.

Lena sometimes gave evidence of having a good deal of spirit, but unfortunately, as her aunt and teacher remarked, in a way that was sadly to her discredit. The first exhibition of this kind was very startling.

Lena was crouched up in a corner one afternoon, with a book in her lap, when her cousin Grace, who was nearly the same age as Lena, asked her to assist in winding some silk. As usual, she was unwilling to oblige, and gruffly refused by saying she was busy reading.

"Sleeping, you mean," said Frank. "I've watched you for the last half hour, and not seen you turn a single leaf."

"No, I was thinking just now, and forgot my book," answered Lena.

"Thinking!" repeated Tom, who was Frank's junior by a year, but far beyond him in ingenuity in giving pain to others at the least possible cost to himself, "Miss Emerson says you can't think."

"I know she does," replied Lena, resignedly.

"I suppose you were thinking last night at Mrs. Poleson's, when you would not dance, nor play at forfeits. But she said you were the most disagreeable little thing she had ever seen in her life."

"Did she?" said Lena, with provoking indifference.

"Yes, and then some one told her you were just like your mamma, who was dreadfully disagreeable too."

In a moment Lena's book was thrown down, and rushing on Tom, who was perched on a high stool before his desk, she dragged him to the ground. A furious battle ensued, in the midst of which Miss Emerson suddenly appeared, and took instant possession of Lena, who it was easy to see was the assailant. For the next hour she was crying quietly on the floor of the darkest room in the house, with its door securely fastened upon her. Now and then an exultant whistle sounded through the keyhole, a performance which she very correctly ascribed to Tom; but she was too unhappy, just then, for it to be in his power to vex her any more. As it grew dark, there was a gentle knock at the door, followed by a few whispered words of comfort.

"Never mind, Lena, you'll be let out in a minute or two."

"But I don't want to get out, Grace," answered Lena, who had recognised the voice. "I would rather stay here."

"O no, you wouldn't; it's wretched being in there. Frank has told mamma that Tom was a coward to say what he did, and so you are going to be let out."

A few minutes after the lock was turned, and Miss Emerson entered the room. "Here, jump up, child," she said, "and let me smooth your hair."

"But I don't want to be let out," persisted Lena, sulkily; "I don't, indeed."

"Nonsense, there is Mr. Archer waiting for you down-stairs—the gentleman who brought you from India. Will you go and see him, or shall I tell him you are naughty, and won't come?"

In an instant Lena had sprung past Miss Emerson, and was hurrying down-stairs. Peeping first into the drawing-room, where she saw only a group of gaily-dressed ladies, and then into the empty breakfast and dining-rooms, she found her visitor, at last, in the study, which had just been vacated by Tom and his tutor. Mr. Archer was too deep in thought to notice her quiet entrance, but he looked up with a smile as she stood in front of him, and drew her kindly to his side.

"I have come to bid you good-bye, Lena," he said. "I leave England next week."

"Oh, how I wish you could take me with you!" said Lena, passionately.

"But I can't, my child; it is best for you to be here. I am leaving many precious ones behind me, but it can't be helped."

He sighed so heavily, that Lena checked her sobs by a strong effort, and asked him quietly how long he should be away.

"Some years, dear; but we must be patient, and do our best wherever our lot lies, till we meet again. When does your aunt go to Fennerton Court?"

"Some time next month," answered Lena, looking up in surprise. "Do you know Fennerton?"

"Yes, my family resides there, dear—my mother and sisters and all my little children. Would you like to see them?"

"O yes, so much, if my aunt will let me."

"I don't think there will be any difficulty about that. My sister has promised to call on you when you are at Fennerton, and take you back with her sometimes. She is very kind, Lena, and I have no doubt you will like her."

Lena felt sure she must like any one belonging to Mr. Archer, but she was too timid to say so. A few minutes after, she had to bid him good-bye, for his remaining time in England was very precious; and then she went back to the dull schoolroom above, trying to comfort herself for the loss of her kind friend by the thought that in three weeks she should be at Fennerton. But those three weeks seemed, as they passed, to drag themselves out into three whole months. Tom teased more than ever, Miss Emerson scolded, and Lena, resenting all her annoyances by fits of sullenness or passion, was generally in disgrace. The packing brought a little diversion. Everybody was too busy to pay much attention to Lena, and she could look on at what was going forward without being much molested. Frank and Tom packed and unpacked their odds and ends about twenty times a day, and kept her busily employed in hunting up lost balls of string, penknives, and other small matters ; but she did not mind that, as every separate time that their precious property was securely corded up seemed to bring the moment of starting to Fennerton a little closer.

"Why, what difference does it make to you where we are ?" asked Tom, one busy morning.

Like most tormentors, he was a quick observer, and Lena's keen interest in the preparations for leaving · Harley Street had not escaped him.

"You won't ride on my pony," he proceeded, "nor go skating on the lake. It will be Miss Emerson and the schoolroom for you there, just as it is here."

"I know that," answered Lena, quietly.

"For some things it will be worse, for there's nobody to give you nice little suppers like Mrs. Poleson and the Brettles."

"But Lena doesn't care for that, Tom," said Frank.

"she isn't so greedy as you are. Here, give me the key of this box. There's a pair of compasses at the bottom that I shall want this afternoon."

"O dear! unpacking again," said Lena, sighing.

That was a process she witnessed most unwillingly; it seemed to throw everything back again.

There was a large dinner party at the Jenyons' the day before the family left for Fennerton Hall. Lena always liked to steal into the dining-room when it was prepared for company, as her uncle was costly in his tastes, and, at all seasons of the year, had his table, on special occasions, richly adorned with fruit and flowers. As she ventured in that evening, and looked admiringly round, Tom's face suddenly peeped from behind a handsome centre-piece that was flashing with lights and brilliantly tinted flowers.

"Come here and look at this bunch of grapes, Lena," said Tom. "Isn't it a beauty?—wouldn't you like it?"

"No," answered Lena; "it wasn't put there for me, so I don't want it."

"Oh, I dare say! You'd rather let old Mosely have it, or that conceited young Poleson, wouldn't you?"

"Yes, if they like. I don't care who gets it."

"Oh, very well! Then you shall have the pleasure of seeing me eat it. Here goes," and Tom stretched across the table.

"If you take it, Tom, I'll tell Miss Emerson," and Lena tried to hold Tom back, but he seized her chubby fingers in his, and obliged them to close on the tempting bunch of grapes. A furious scuffle ensued. Tom and Lena pushed and pulled; the massive centre-piece rocked to and fro, and at last came down with a great crash, scattering ruin all around it. Tom and Lena fell back aghast at the catastrophe, and looked at each other in affright.

"O Tom! how could you?" gasped Lena.

"How could *you*, you mean," returned Tom.

He had quite recovered his self-possession by that time, and was looking in innocent unconcern at the mischief he had caused, when his mamma and Miss Emerson hurried into the room, followed by one or two servants.

"O Tom, Tom! what have you done?" said Mrs. Jenyon, who did not at first perceive Lena.

"It was Lena," replied Tom; "she wanted to get a bunch of grapes."

"I did not," said Lena, sullenly; "you wanted them."

"What were you pulling at them for, then, if you didn't want them?"

"Because you held my hand and made me. I couldn't prevent it."

"A likely story," said Tom. "What should I want a cat's paw for?—the dish wasn't hot."

This line of argument was deemed conclusive, and Lena was led to the dark room up-stairs in sad disgrace.

The next day she had one of her sullen fits, and refused to add anything to the explanation she had already given. Frank was the only one who stood up for her; but his championship was conducted in such a very off-hand manner, that Lena did not in the least thank him for it. He believed her version of the affair, he said; for, disagreeable as she was, he had never found her guilty of greediness or story-telling, while Tom was constantly being convicted of both. However, Tom maintained his innocence so stoutly, that he came off the conqueror; and on the morning after the arrival of the family at Fennerton Court he was careering round the park on his pony, while Lena was still a prisoner in Miss Emerson's custody.

"I think you had better beg your aunt's pardon," said Miss Emerson; "you will get nothing by holding out."

"I haven't done anything wrong," answered Lena; "there is nothing to be forgiven."

"But your aunt is the best judge of that, and she thinks there is. Come, don't be a foolish child; it isn't very pleasant to be in disgrace."

"I don't mind when there is no cause for it," answered Lena, sturdily.

But a day or two after, when she heard that one of her aunt's visitors, who, she felt sure, must be Miss Archer, had asked to see her, and been told that she was in disgrace, and could not be allowed to come down, Lena felt that punishment, whether merited or not, is a very bitter thing indeed.

After that, her imagination was constantly suggesting disagreeable probabilities. Among the worst was a fear that, having heard such a bad account of her on her first visit, Miss Archer would never ask for her again; and that Mr. Archer might one day hear of her naughtiness, and feel glad that his little children had never known her. A dreary week followed, and then Lena's

position grew less unpleasant. Though not quite restored to favour, she was again allowed to share some
of her cousin Grace's privileges.

One evening Mrs. Jenyon was receiving some friends,
and Lena, with her two elder cousins, went down for
a short time to the drawing-room. Tom, on account of
some misdemeanour, was kept back—a mode of punishment which he resented highly, but which Lena, being
very shy of strangers, would have been glad to share.
As soon as she could contrive to escape, she stole away
into an adjoining conservatory—a pleasant retreat,
bright with gay flowers, and lit up here and there
by softly glowing lamps. The place had special at-
tractions for Lena. No tormentor's face was likely to
peer from behind any of the green foliage, for neither
Frank nor Tom was much given to solitary meditation ;
and besides the luxury of being able to wander about
unmolested, she could enjoy the sight of many well-
known plants, that seemed like old friends. At the
further end of the conservatory was a snug little bench,
and there Lena sat down, intending to stay till Miss
Emerson, who was in the secret of her hiding-place,
came to fetch her.

Presently there was a soft rustle of silk close behind
her, and, looking round, she saw a lady with a sweet
grave face.

"Are you Lena Halcot ?" asked the lady, holding
out her hand.

"Yes, ma'am." And Lena jumped up, flushing and
trembling with eager anticipation. "Could this be
Miss Archer ? "

The question was answered by the young lady taking Lena in her arms, and kissing her tenderly. "Can you make room for me on your seat?" asked Miss Archer.

Lena gathered her white skirts into the smallest possible compass, and then nestled closely up to her new friend.

" I was afraid you would never try to see me again," she said.

" Why not, Lena?"

" Because you heard before of my being so naughty. But it was Tom who wanted the grapes, and broke the centre-piece ; it was indeed."

" Then I hope he has explained all that."

" No, he hasn't ; he's a wicked story-telling boy, and I hate him."

" O my poor child," said Miss Archer, softly.

" Why do you pity me?" asked Lena, who felt conscious of not deserving much compassion just then.

" Because you say such very shocking things. But now tell me how all this happened?"

Lena gave a truthful version of the affair, and then Miss Archer asked whether Tom's word was generally relied on in the household.

" No ; everybody knows he is a story-teller."

" And you have not the same character, I hope, Lena?"

" O dear, no. Frank said he believed me, for I always spoke the truth."

" And was he the only one who took your part?"

" Yes, and he did it so unkindly that I would rather he had not interfered at all."

"Then I am afraid, Lena, that you have not any friends in the household," said Miss Archer, gravely.

"No, not one ; everybody is unkind to me."

"That is a very sad state of things ! Are you quite sure that it has been brought about without any fault on your side ? Think a little, dear, before you answer me."

Lena obeyed, and then said honestly, "Perhaps not, but I don't see how it is to be helped."

"Listen to me, Lena. In olden times people never liked to venture empty-handed into the presence of any one from whom they hoped to obtain some favour. Sometimes their gift was poor, sometimes it was rich, according to their means. You remember, I dare say, that the sons of Jacob took a present to the powerful governor of Egypt, and the wise men of the East presented gifts to the infant Saviour. I am afraid, Lena, you came among your unknown friends here without your offering."

"But I hadn't anything to bring, Miss Archer."

"O yes, you had, dear, if you had been willing to offer it ; something so precious that money could not buy it."

"I don't know what it could be."

"Then I must help you to find out. Why were you so glad to see me just now ; did you think I had brought you a very handsome present ?"

"O no, I shouldn't have cared for that at all."

"But you expected something, what was it ? "

"I hoped you would like me, and be kind to me."

"That I should bring you a little store of love. So

then, Lena, a pleasant offering can be made that does not cost us anything. Wouldn't it have been easy to bring that to your new friends?"

"Yes, if they had been kind to me."

"Oh, the kindness would have come in due time. Those wise men of old presented their gifts first, and then waited patiently till the favour they desired was granted them. You must follow the same plan, Lena."

"But not with every one, Miss Archer. I can't love Tom, who is always teasing me, and getting me into trouble."

"Well, not all at once, I dare say. But what do you generally do when he teases you? Tell me quite truthfully."

"Sometimes I feel sulky," Lena murmured, "and sometimes I get into a dreadful passion."

"Well, suppose, instead of doing either, you try to take his teasing gently. Do you think that will be very difficult to manage?"

"Yes, I am sure it will; and, besides, it won't be loving him, Miss Archer."

"But it will be a first step towards it, and towards making him love you too. However, we can talk about this another time, Lena, for your aunt has promised to let you spend to-morrow with me."

"Oh, thank you; and is Grace to go too?"

"No, I must have you quite by yourself on your first visit, for I have so much to talk about, and so many new friends to whom I wish to introduce you. And now, I think, we must not stay here any longer. Will you come back with me?"

E

"Oh, I like being here so much best, Miss Archer."

"But it is not good for you, Lena, nor right, to mope by yourself. Come, I am not going to leave you behind."

They went back to the drawing-room together, and very soon after Lena was summoned away by Miss Emerson. Tom was in hiding somewhere on the stairs to make a few faces at her as she passed ; but in her quiet room she soon felt quite happy again, and lay awake some time thinking of the pleasant visit she was to pay on the morrow.

But the day began, as wished-for days often do, a little inauspiciously. Tom was ill-tempered at having seen Lena promoted to favour in his place, and her evident satisfaction at her approaching visit to the Archers was in his estimation a further aggravation of his wrongs. Just before she started he took an opportunity of soothing his wrathful feelings in a way peculiar to himself.

"So you're going out all alone to-day, Lena," he said; "isn't that grand !"

"I don't know," Lena answered, soberly, not quite liking the twinkle in Tom's eye. "But you or Grace will go with me next time, I dare say."

"Oh, shall we ? that's a likely thing !"

"Yes, I know Miss Archer means to ask you."

"Does she ? it's very obliging of her, I'm sure ! But the thing will be to get us to go."

"I don't expect there'll be much difficulty about that," answered Lena.

"Oh, then, you've got to find out your mistake. Mamma says the Archers are not visitable people."

"Then why did she ask Miss Archer here to dinner yesterday?"

"Oh, because it couldn't be helped, I suppose. But Miss Archer's coming to us and our going to see her are two very different things."

"You are telling dreadful stories now! You know she is quite as good as any one here."

"Oh, is she? Well, Blake told me the other day that Miss Archer and her mother dig up their garden, and wait on themselves at dinner."

Lena did not know that they might do both and yet be ladies at the same time; so, as the only way of maintaining their dignity, she denied the charge with great vehemence.

"Ah, well, you'll see," said Tom. "I'd advise you to wear your oldest frock, and take a pinafore, for they'll soon set you to work."

Lena's passion was just getting quite beyond her own control, when Miss Emerson fortunately entered the room, and restored order.

An hour after, Lena stood with swollen eyelids at the door of the Archers' cottage. Miss Archer came out to receive her, looking, Lena thought, nicer than on the previous evening, though her handsome silk dress was exchanged for a plain cotton one. She led Lena up-stairs to a small neat chamber, bright with white draperies and richly-tinted autumn flowers.

"I am afraid you have been in trouble this morning, dear," she said, as she took off Lena's hat, and carefully smoothed her hair. "But never mind, we'll talk about it by-and-by. I want you to come and see my school now."

"I didn't know you had one," answered Lena in surprise.

"But you have heard of my scholars, I am sure; they are my brother John's children, Lena. We have not finished our lessons yet, but you can come with me if you like and see how we get on."

Lena did not feel at all obliged to Miss Archer for the permission, and followed her very reluctantly, fearing she should soon see cause to grow terribly afraid of her. The schoolroom into which she was conducted, however, was not at all alarming in its aspect. There were pleasant pictures on the walls instead of maps, and not a single form or high stool to be seen; but Lena found soon after that the apartment was used as dining-room as well, a circumstance that accounted for the absence of all customary schoolroom decorations. Six children, varying in age from thirteen to four, were seated round the long centre table. They all rose as Lena entered the room, and came one after the other to shake hands with her. She knew the name of each, and, to some extent, the character too, for those children had been a never-failing topic of conversation between Mr. Archer and herself during their long journey from India.

"And now we have only our object lesson," said Miss Archer, as she took her place at the head of her little class. "Come, let me see what you have brought to-day."

"It was my turn to choose, Aunt Ellen," said the youngest child ; "it's Saturday, you know."

"So it is, Johnny. Lena," and Miss Archer turned to her little guest, "the children take turns in choosing the subject of the lesson. Mary, being the eldest, has her choice on Monday, Harry on Tuesday, and so we go on till we get to Johnny and Saturday. Now, then, what have you brought us ?"

There was a hearty chorus of laughter as the little fellow, after a good deal of fumbling in the depths of his pocket, suddenly produced a lump of sugar.

"A capital subject for a lesson, Johnny," said Miss Archer. "Harry, pass it up."

The piece of sugar was placed before Miss Archer, and then followed between teacher and pupils a rapid interchange of question and answer. Lena listened with eager attention, but did not quite know whether they were in fun or earnest. Now and then a question was addressed to her, but, fortunately, whenever she hesitated so many voices were raised to answer it, that her ignorance respecting the antecedents of the lump of sugar passed unnoticed. However, before the lesson was over she had heard the whole history of it, from its first existence in the tall Indian cane, to its last adventures at the hands of the London sugar-bakers.

"Now, children," said Miss Archer, rising, "you may get ready for your walk. And Johnny, here is your lump of sugar."

"May I eat it, aunt ?"

"Yes ; I am glad you had the self-denial to keep it all the morning untouched in your pocket."

As soon as the children were gone, Miss Archer turned to Lena and asked her how she had liked the object lesson.

"It was like play," answered Lena.

"Well, I am glad you thought it pleasant. I always find it necessary to have it after everything else is finished, as we are apt to get a little riotous over it. But why did you say the lesson was like play, Lena? Don't you often find work quite as pleasant as play?"

"No, never," answered Lena bluntly, "I don't like it."

Miss Archer looked gravely at her, but seeing that she looked more careworn than sullen or idle, she said kindly, "Perhaps it has never been made pleasant to you, dear."

Before going out, Lena was taken into the drawing-room to see Mrs. Archer—a grave, delicate-looking lady, of whom she felt at first rather in awe; and then the little party started on their ramble.

Just beyond the village of Fennerton there was a wide, pleasant heath, over which Master Tom was very fond of careering on his pony, but which Lena had only seen occasionally from the carriage window. She was very glad when she found the walk was to lie in that direction, and kept on happily at Miss Archer's side. A pause was made at more than one cottage door as they passed through the village, to inquire after an old person or sick child, and leave some little dainty that had been entrusted, so far, to Johnny's care. At last the heath was reached, and the little Archers scampered off in all directions, leaving Miss Archer and Lena to follow more leisurely.

"And now tell me what was troubling you this morning, Lena," said Miss Archer.

"Oh, it was Tom," murmured Lena.

"Why, what was he teasing you about?"

"Oh don't ask me Miss Archer, please; I would so much rather not say."

"I am sorry for that, Lena," said Miss Archer, gravely.

"No, no, I don't mean that I have been naughtier than usual—I shouldn't mind telling you of that; but it was some things Tom said that I would rather not repeat."

"Oh, is that all? well, we'll let them pass. They were very provoking speeches, I dare say, but I hope you tried to take them patiently."

"At first I did, but he got worse and worse;" and, after some hesitation, Lena recounted all that had passed between herself and Tom that morning, adding that "she knew his assertions were all stories, and had told him so."

"But you knew nothing of the kind, dear; so it was very foolish and wrong to contradict. Tom was quite right, I do work in my garden, and very hard, sometimes."

"Do you? we thought ladies never did such things?"

"Why not? Do you and Tom fancy that they ought to sit in their drawing-rooms all day and receive company? That is a great mistake, Lena; some ladies are obliged to work very hard indeed. It is easy to be idle and useless, you know."

"Yes; but Miss Emerson always tells Grace and me that we are unlady-like if we do anything out of the way."

"And she is quite right—doing anything out of our way is not certainly at all becoming. If I kept a gardener, Lena, it would be very unlady-like in me to take his work out of his hands; but as I do not, I would rather attend to our garden myself than see it untidy. Don't you think that far the best way?"

Lena supposed it must be, as Miss Archer said so, but still she felt a good deal puzzled.

As the day wore on, she heard and saw a great many things to surprise her. The Archers' household was a very busy one. Every one in it had special duties to attend to, from Mrs. Archer, who sat at the pleasant drawing-room window with her large work-basket before her, to Johnny, who trotted about the house on small errands. There was but one servant to attend to the family wants, and she was old, and needed, Miss Archer said, to be spared as much as possible. Yet there were no signs of confusion anywhere. Everything went forward in quite as orderly a way as at Fennerton Court, and in Lena's estimation, far more pleasantly.

Before leaving, Lena was taken into a bedroom adjoining Miss Archer's, and exactly like it in every respect, except having a better supply of books.

"This is my brother's room," said Miss Archer. "I always come here when I feel studious. It is Harry's work to dust all these books every day, and Mary attends to the flowers. You see she keeps a good supply here."

"But what is the use of taking so much trouble now Mr. Archer is away?" asked Lena.

"Well, that is not an easy question to answer; I think we do it all entirely for our own satisfaction. Both Mary and Harry would think their day's happiness incomplete if they had left their duties in their papa's room undone. Come and look at this fern, Lena; we found it in one of our rambles.

They were bending over the plant and intently examining its delicate spray-like leaves, when a gentle knock was heard· at the door, and a chubby face peeped in.

"What is it, Johnny?" asked Miss Archer.

"A great boy come for Lena, and he says he can't wait."

Lena hurried on her hat and cloak, and then lifted her face in silence to Miss Archer.

"Can't you look brighter than that, dear?" said Miss Archer, as she gave her the expected kiss; "your friends will think you have not had a happy day."

"O no, they won't notice me, Miss Archer. But I can't feel happy that I am going back to them again."

"Have you thought of what we were talking about last night?"

"Of the offering? O yes; but it is no use trying; you heard how I began this morning."

"But that was only one failure; you may get on better another time. But I think you know what you must do if you would succeed in the end, Lena ; for my brother told me you had been very carefully taught."

"O yes, but all that seems gone now. I never read or pray as I used to, for Tom and Grace always laugh at me."

"Never mind that ; persevere steadily, and they will respect you in the end for your patient continuance in well-doing. But I am not surprised, Lena, at your having found your cousin's teasing so hard to bear if prayer and Bible-reading have been neglected. Without a little sunshine in our own hearts, you know, we cannot brighten the dark things about us."

"No, I will try to do better, Miss Archer, I will, indeed."

They said good-bye again ; and then Lena ran downstairs. Outside the gate she found Tom, mounted on his pony.

"You'll have to get on at a fine rate, Lena," he said, "if you mean to keep up with me."

An angry retort was on Lena's lips, but she checked it, and answered gently,

"Very well, Tom, I'll walk as fast as I can."

Tom drew in his rein a little, and looked at her in surprise.

"Going out seems to have done you good," he said, "and sent you home better tempered. I suppose you've had a fine time."

"Yes, I have indeed."

"Well, I only wish I'd had the luck to be out of the way, too, for we've had a grand upset at home.

Grace has something the matter with her, and Ma has had to send to town for old Mosely."

"O Tom, I hope it isn't anything bad. Is she very ill?"

"I don't know. The rest of us have been kept close together under Miss Emerson's wing all day; and she hasn't made herself pleasant company, I can tell you."

Lena walked very sorrowfully home. Of all her cousins she certainly liked Grace the best. She was almost as fond of teasing as Tom, but had more honesty of character; and, just then, Lena could recollect nothing but her good-natured interference in her behalf occasionally when she was in disgrace.

On reaching home, almost the first person she saw was her Aunt Jenyon, who looked pale and anxious.

"Is Grace better, aunt?" she asked.

"No, dear, not yet; but the doctor says she is going on very well."

"May I go and see her?"

"Not now, dear; her illness is something catching, we fear, and I cannot have you all laid up together. Good-night;" and Mrs. Jenyon kissed Lena more kindly than usual.

The following week Tom was taken ill; and a few mornings after that Lena announced to Miss Emerson that she did not feel quite well, and wanted to keep in bed.

"Dear me, how very tiresome!" said Miss Emerson; "we shall have you to nurse now."

"But I won't give you much trouble, Miss Emerson; I shall be very quiet."

"Well, I hope you will, and then you'll get well all the sooner. Does your head ache?"

"Yes, very much, and the light hurts my eyes."

Miss Emerson drew the curtains of the bed closer round her; and resigned herself to divide her attentions for the next few days between Tom's room and Lena's.

A few hours later, Lena was roused from sleep by a light step at her bedside, and Miss Archer's hand gently put back the curtains.

"Oh, how kind of you to come," said Lena, lifting up her flushed face to be kissed. "But is it quite safe? Dr. Moseley wouldn't let me go near Tom nor Grace."

"There is no fear, dear; I shall take a good run on the heath before going back. Should you like to see me every day till you get well?"

"O yes; only it will be giving you so much trouble."

"Not the least. I shall send the children home with Mary, who is quite old enough to take care of them, and then come on to you. And now tell me how you are; Miss Emerson says you were not taken ill till this morning."

"Yes, my head was aching very much all day yesterday, but I thought it would get better again."

"Then all you have to do now is to keep quite still, and mind all Miss Emerson tells you."

Lena promised to do both; and then lay listening for some time with charmed ears to Miss Archer's pleasant account of some of her busy home doings that morning. Before leaving, she reminded Lena of the promise she had made her some days before to be more diligent in Bible reading and prayer.

"O yes, I haven't forgotten that," answered Lena ; "but I cannot read now; it would make my eyes ache so."

"Then I must help you to keep your promise, dear, until you get well again ;" and, taking a small Testament from her pocket, Miss Archer read a small portion aloud. Then, kneeling for a few minutes at the bedside, she pleaded for the sick child in words that she could easily follow.

Lena bore her illness very patiently. She was naturally a quiet child ; and to feel herself quite secure from Tom's teasing, and have Miss Archer to see her every day, was ample compensation for all her sufferings. As she grew better, the Bible reading, and the conversations that followed it, were considerably extended; and Lena made steady progress under Miss Archer's daily teaching.

"I think I shall find it quite easy to make my offering now," said Lena, one morning, to Miss Archer.

"What makes you fancy that, dear ? "

"Because I feel it will be pleasant. I always knew that I ought to love everybody ; but it seemed as if it must be such hard work, that I never liked to begin."

"I think you had allowed your love to your Saviour to grow cold, Lena, and that made you find it so difficult to obey Him. When we love Him truly, we soon see that 'His commandments are not grievous.' "

"I must think of that if I ever get angry with Tom again," answered Lena.

The strength of her good resolutions was soon tested. Tom had been ranging the house for some days in recovered health, and that afternoon, in defiance of Miss Emerson's express commands, he stole into Lena's room.

"O Tom!" said Lena, looking up in dismay, "are you well enough to be about again?"

"Yes, you're glad to see me, ain't you?" answered Tom, with a grimace. "Come, I'm going to cheer you up a bit; it's dull being alone."

"O no, it isn't, Tom. I like it best; I do, indeed."

"Well, that's polite; but I shan't take offence. Look here, *I* want to be amused, if you don't; so you've got to read that while I mend my ship."

Lena took the book Tom thrust into her hand, and then looked on sorrowfully while he pushed her pretty toilet ornaments unceremoniously aside to make room for his ship, and half the boy's litter contained in his pockets.

"Now, then," said Tom, as he applied himself to his work, "when are you going to begin?"

"But I can't read, Tom, my eyes are too weak."

"Well, using them a little will do them good; just you see if it don't. Here, I'll show you where I left off, and then you may set to work at once."

Tom found the place, and then Lena, very slowly and reluctantly, began her task.

"Come, get on faster than that," said Tom, "and louder, too. Who's to hear you, I should like to know?"

"But I don't like the book, Tom; it isn't a nice one."

"Never you mind that, *I* like it. Come, now, it will be all the worse for you if you make yourself disagreeable."

Lena felt herself so entirely in his power that she wisely made no further resistance. Voice and sight were exerted to the utmost till Miss Emerson came in, when she suddenly broke down, and sank back white and sobbing on her pillow.

"Well, now," said Tom, with an injured look, "that's a fine way to behave when people take the trouble to come and amuse you."

"You've no business here, Tom," said Miss Emerson, sharply. "Go away directly, and take all this rubbish with you."

Tom obeyed with great promptness; and Lena's nervous tremor was quieted by Miss Emerson's promise to keep a stricter watch over his movements for the next few days.

On seeing Miss Archer again, Lena told her of Tom's unwelcome visit, and its unfortunate termination.

"I don't think I was very cross," said Lena, humbly, "but I couldn't help crying."

"Well, we must make some allowance for your not being very strong, and Tom was certainly rather unmerciful. Perhaps he only comes here tormenting you for want of something better to do. I'll ask Miss Emerson to send him round to us occasionally, and we'll find him plenty of work."

"Oh, pray don't, Miss Archer; you can't think how naughty he is."

"O yes, I can; and that is why I want to see him

thoroughly busy. I'll speak to Miss Emerson about it to-day, as I pass the schoolroom."

Rather late that evening, Tom put his head into Lena's room with far more circumspection than he usually displayed in any of his proceedings, and asked her if he might venture any further.

"I don't know, Tom; what do you want?"

"Well, I've something to give you, so you'd better say Yes."

The certainty that he would please himself in any case induced Lena to yield; and then Tom came in, bringing a bunch of flowers, which he tossed down unceremoniously on her bed.

"O Tom, these came from the Archers!" said Lena, as she recognised, between some dark chrysanthemums, a few sprays of the delicate fern she had seen in Mr. Archer's room.

"Yes; I've been there all the afternoon weeding. What do you think of that?"

"Well, I am very glad, if you liked it. Did Miss Archer set you to work?"

"Yes; you should have seen her do it. She knows how to order about; but I like her all the better for that. But the best of all," continued Tom, flushing up a little, "was when I told Harry he might come and have a ride on my pony sometimes, thinking to do him a great favour. And she turned sharp round with, 'We don't know much about you yet, Tom; wait till we're better acquainted, and then, if we get on together as I hope we shall, Harry can go and see you as often as you like.' Fancy her talking to me like that!"

Page 89

"But it was quite right, wasn't it ?"

"I don't know ; I thought all the obligation on the other side. However, it don't much matter," and Tom turned away, whistling.

"Good-night, Tom," said Lena, holding out her hand, "and thank you for bringing me these."

"Oh, you're wonderfully good all at once ! I wonder how long that's going to last ?"

"All my life, I hope, Tom. I am very sorry for having been passionate when you teased me, and never mean to be so any more, if I can help it."

"Why, what's put that in your head? who's been complaining of you ?"

"Nobody. I know I've been wrong myself, but you'll help me to do better, won't you ?"

"Oh, come, don't look like that," said Tom, "or there'll be no fun in plaguing you."

"But I don't want there to be any, Tom ; I want to be friends."

"So we are," answered Tom ; "what's the use of making a fuss ?" However, though he was not to be betrayed into any amicable demonstration, Lena soon began to find out that her simple offering—her look and word of love—had won for her some favour even in Master Tom's eyes.

A few days after, Lena was able to go down-stairs again, and resume some of her duties with Miss Emerson, but Grace was still too ill to leave her room. Nearly another week passed before Lena was permitted to go in and see her little cousin, and then she was shocked at the change that had taken place in her.

F

"Oh, how ill you have been!" said Lena, kneeling down by the side of Grace's low couch; "I wish they had let me come and see you sooner."

"But you have been ill, too," answered Grace. "Wasn't it dreadfully dull to be shut up all alone with Miss Emerson?"

"O no; Miss Archer came to me every day, and read to me."

"Did she? I wish she would come and see me. What did she read?"

"The Bible."

"Oh, but that is only for Sundays, and sick people who are going to die. Wouldn't she read me story-books?"

"No, I don't think she could find time, for she has so much to do; but I'll read you stories if you like."

"O yes, so Frank said, and got tired in less than half-an-hour."

"But I can keep on as long as you like; you shall see."

Before Lena's powers began to fail, Grace was fast asleep; but Lena was too much interested in her book to find it out, till the rustling of her aunt's dress close beside her made her look up.

"This is very kind of you, Lena," said Mrs. Jenyon, kissing her softly; "I haven't seen Grace in such a quiet sleep for a long while. I think I can trust you now to come and see her every day, if you won't find it dull."

"Oh! thank you, aunt, I shall like it very much."

So after that, as soon as her studies were over with

Miss Emerson, Lena always hurried up to sit with Grace. Sometimes she read or talked to her, and sometimes, when Grace was not so well, she kept quietly near, watching and soothing her.

" Are you quite sure all is right with Lena ? " Mrs. Jenyon asked one day of Dr. Mosely. " She seems so much altered since her illness."

" Oh, there is nothing the matter with her now, replied the doctor, laying his hand kindly on Lena's head. " I think it is her nature to be quiet."

But Mrs. Jenyon did not seem quite satisfied, and still watched Lena occasionally a little uneasily. However, Lena's increased happiness in the love she was giving and receiving soon brightened her looks so much, that there seemed no cause for any further anxiety on her account.

As the autumn days grew chilly, and Grace was still very delicate, it was arranged that Mrs. Jenyon should take her to spend some days in Devonshire. Lena begged earnestly to be allowed to accompany them, but Mrs. Jenyon hesitated for some time about granting her request, for she knew that Lena's attentions to Grace must be paid at a considerable amount of self-sacrifice, for the poor child was often sadly exacting and hard to please.

" I don't like you to lose your studies, Lena," said Mrs. Jenyon, " for we may not be back for a long while."

" Oh, never mind, they can wait, aunt, till Grace gets well, and then we'll both work hard together."

" And how will you get on without your kind friend, Miss Archer ? you haven't thought about that."

"O yes, I have, but she doesn't want me, and Grace does."

"Very well, dear," answered her aunt at last; "you shall go, though it seems hardly right to take you. But you will be a great comfort to me."

Willingly as the sacrifice was made, Lena went very sorrowfully to pay her farewell visit to the Archers. The pleasant tea in the little dining-room was lingered over as long as possible; and then Lena sat for a while alone with Miss Archer, nestling to her very closely when she thought that a whole year might pass before she saw her again. Miss Archer comforted her as well as she could, and then began to inquire about Grace.

"She is very hard to please," said Lena, who saw the dark side of everything just then; "I don't know what to do to amuse her sometimes."

"I hardly wonder at that, dear; mere amusement becomes very wearisome after a while. Can't you give her anything better?"

"She won't let me; she says the Bible is only for Sundays and sick people."

"But you know better, Lena, and must tell her so."

"Yes, I will try. But I don't like to vex her—I want so much to make her like me."

"And the best way to succeed, dear, is to try to make her happy in the right way."

Lena promised to do her best, and then took her leave.

On the following day she left for Devonshire with her aunt and cousin, and the next few weeks were spent in wandering from place to place on the pleasant coast.

The time passed far more agreeably than Lena had expected. Her aunt seemed to grow daily more motherly towards her, and, if any little difficulty arose, a long letter from Miss Archer was sure to set all right. Grace, too, mended rapidly, and before Christmas she was quite strong enough to return home. So they came, but not to Harley Street, as Lena had expected. Fennerton Court was put into holiday trim to receive them; and in the hall, with Tom, Harry, and a perfect forest of holly-berries around her, stood Miss Archer, to give them a hearty welcome.

Seeing so many old friends again, and being made much of, as people are when they have been away for a little while, was very delightful; but Lena's happiness was not quite complete till she got Miss Archer all to herself, in a quiet corner, to discuss some of the pleasant matters she had already communicated to her over and over again in her letters.

"You can't think how nice our Bible readings are now, Miss Archer," was her first whispered remark; "Gracie never gets tired of them."

"And you haven't lost your friend, Lena, by being faithful?"

"O no! we get on much more happily together. But then they are all so good; even Tom wrote to me sometimes—queer letters, that will make you laugh; but then he meant them to be kind."

"I am glad of that; you thought Tom would be so very hard to conciliate."

"But he wasn't ; he came round at once."

"Ah, and so would all our tiresome friends, I expect, Lena, if we went the right way to work with them. It's wonderful what a little love will do."

"Yes," answered Lena, absently.

She was considering what confidential topic she should enter on next; but, before she had decided, Tom plunged into the snug corner with a load of stereoscopic slides for Miss Archer's inspection, and the tête-à-tête was broken up.

"It's all very fine talking," said Tom, "but I always like something to do."

Fortunately the "something" was not exclusively confined to teasing now. Tom was quite tamed, and there was no longer any necessity to fly off out of his way, or keep on the defensive when he was by. It would be a great relief to everybody if all the disagreeable mischievous Toms were put down in the same way.

THE QUIET WITNESS.

"Even a child is known by his doings, whether his work be
pure, and whether it be right"—Prov. xx. 11.

SCHOOL was over, and boys and girls came trooping
down the lane towards the village. Right in their path
was a rough-looking, ill-clad boy of twelve or thirteen,
who was stretched· at full length on the ground, idly
pulling at the long tufts of grass within his reach.
Only one of the school children, a little girl, who
seemed to be the youngest of the party, stopped to
speak to him as she passed. But her hand was rudely
grasped by a stout elder sister, who said sharply—

"Come away, Nancy ; it's Jem Hazel."

"Yes, I know ; but I want to ask him why he
doesn't go home. I don't like to see him lie there."

"But he's a bad boy, and mother says we're not to
speak to him," and the little girl was hurried on with
the rest of her companions.

As soon as they were all out of sight Jem scrambled
to his feet, and went up the lane towards the school.
On his way he overtook a shining beetle, travelling
leisurely along without appearing to be troubled with
any fears as to its own safety. He examined it for
some time attentively, and then put it, with great care,
in a sheltered nook under the hedge. Jem Hazel

could not have been a very bad boy, or he would not have cared whose foot crushed the poor beetle.

Finding no one in the wide schoolroom, Jem went round to the back of the house, and came suddenly upon the open door of a small neat kitchen, in which the master and his wife were comfortably sipping their tea.

" Well, Jem," said the master, kindly, " come in, and tell us what you want."

Jem entered the kitchen very readily, but seemed to find some difficulty in stating his business. At last it came—

" Please, sir, I want to be taught."

" Why, what has put that in your head, Jem ?"

" I don't know, sir; it's been there a long while."

" Did your mother send you ?"

" No, sir, I came of myself."

"Then I must see your mother about it, my boy, and hear what she says."

" Oh! she's willing for me to come, sir, only I've got to find the money for the books and schooling myself. But I'll do it somehow."

" Somehow ?" repeated the master, gravely ; "it must come honestly, you know, Jem."

Jem coloured a little, and then answered quietly, " I meant that, sir."

" Well, I think you did, for you look like an honest boy. There, you may come to-morrow morning, and I'll see what you can do."

" I work at Farmer Neal's in the morning, sir; mother can't do without that."

" Then you'll only have the rest of the day for your schooling, Jem, and to earn the pence to pay for it. I'm afraid you are undertaking too much."

" No, sir, I'm not," Jem answered respectfully, " I can do it."

" Very well ; you can try, at all events, and if you succeed, your learning will seem more precious than if you had come by it easily."

Jem thanked the master, but did not seemed disposed to go. After looking for a few moments into the crown of his ragged cap, he asked if he might have a book to read at home, as he had heard that volumes were sometimes lent to the children from the school library.

" Certainly," answered the master, " I am glad you can read, Jem. Come with me, and take any book you like best."

Jem followed the master into the schoolroom, but the sight of several rows of books ranged one over the other seemed greatly to perplex him.

" Perhaps you'll choose for me, sir," said Jem ; " I don't know which to take."

" What sort of book would you like ? "

" One with pictures, sir," was the only preference Jem seemed able to give.

So the difficulty of selection being greatly simplified, the master put a neatly covered book into his hand, telling him to keep it clean, and bring it back as soon as he had read it. Jem thanked the master, took his book, and ran off briskly homewards. On his way he stopped occasionally to try to find out the contents of his book—an inquiry in which he was greatly assisted by the pictures. One of these pauses was made just outside the vicarage, and, as he was starting off again, he heard his own name softly uttered, and, looking round, saw a bright little face peeping over the gate behind him.

"Jem, Jem, where did you get that book ? Have you been to the school ?"

"Yes, Miss Mary," answered Jem, standing respectfully before his little questioner ; "and the master says I may begin to-morrow."

"Oh, I am so glad ! And now you must come and look at my tulips ; they are just beginning to flower," and Miss Mary seized one of Jem's ragged cuffs and dragged him into the garden.

While they were admiring the flowers, Mr. Bracy little Mary's papa, stepped out of his study window, and was instantly told, as a most exciting piece of intelligence, that Jem was going to school the next day.

"But can your mother spare you, my man ? " said the vicar. " You are getting a great boy now, and ought to be helping her."

" So I do, sir ; I shall still keep on at Farmer Neal's in the morning, and I'm going to ask him to give me a little extra work, now and then, to pay for my books and schooling."

"Then you have promised Mr. Dunn the weekly pence without knowing where they were to come from, Jem ? "

" I hoped I should get them somehow, sir."

" But you were not sure. That was not strictly

honest, Jem ; you should never incur a debt unless you are quite certain of having the means to pay it. Suppose Mr. Neal refuses the extra work—what will you do ? "

" Give up going to the school, sir," answered Jem, sorrowfully.

" O papa, don't let him do that ! " said little Mary. " Pay the pence for him."

" Shall I, Jem ? "

" No sir, thank you," replied Jem, respectfully, " I would rather earn them."

" Very well, so you shall. What time do you leave Mr. Neal's ? "

" Half-past twelve, sir."

" Then that gives you an hour and a half to yourself before school opens, so I think you may manage to spend a third of that time in my garden. The paths sadly want a little attention, as you see, Jem, and if you keep them tolerably clear of weeds, you shall have your school pence, and whatever you need over for a book now and then."

Jem thanked the vicar gratefully, and went on his way with a mind considerably relieved.

The next day he entered on his round of duties. At school he found, at first, a good deal to perplex him. He was awkward in handling his slate, and though he could get at the sense of a page of print very well when he studied it in some quiet corner alone, he scarcely managed to say half-a-dozen words correctly when he stood up for his reading lesson in the midst of a whole class of boys. The treatment he met with in the lane, too, the afternoon before, was repeated, with additional aggravations, but being a quiet lad, and eager for self-improvement, he bore his vexations patiently, and felt, after his first afternoon at school was over, as steady as ever in his determination to persevere.

When Jem and the other school-children were gone, Nat Pilcher, a boy of about Jem's age, lingered behind, walking slowly up and down the room, and glancing from time to time at the master, who was standing at his desk examining a pile of copy books.

"Well, Nat," said Mr. Dunn, looking up, "what are you waiting for?"

"Please, sir, I want to speak to you about Jem Hazel."

"Oh, indeed. And what have you got to say about him?"

"Nothing particular, only his father, sir."

"His father! we'll keep to Jem, if you please. Do you know anything against him?"

"No, sir," answered Nat, looking a little disconcerted; "but I suppose he isn't much good, for mother told me I wasn't to speak to him."

"Very well, obey your mother. Jem Hazel comes here to learn, and the less you talk to him the faster he'll get on."

The master was very angry; but, when he had had time to think the matter over, he determined to put it in a better light to his scholars, and, as soon as they were assembled the next day, he got into his desk, and held up his hand to command silence and attention.

"Boys," he said, "there was a fierce bird once who was a sad torment to his neighbours. It does not matter now what he did, but he fell so quickly from bad to worse, that at last they all rose up against him, and drove him to a far-off country, where he could never annoy them any more. After he was gone it was found that he had left a poor little nestling behind, and all the birds of the place were sadly perplexed as to what they should do with it. Some said, 'he comes of a bad stock, and the less we meddle with him the better;' but one grave old owl said—'Suppose we wait and see how he behaves. If he does wrong we can easily punish him as we did his father, but if he is disposed to live peaceably among us, it would not be just in us to prevent it. Let us give him a chance.'

"Now, boys, we must not be harder in our judgment than the old owl in my fable. Jem Hazel comes of a bad stock, I know, but he may turn out a good honest lad for all that. Just let us see what witness his own conduct bears of him before we condemn him. I have heard that some of your mothers have told you not to speak to him. They do quite right to keep you out of bad company; but if Jem shows himself the steady lad I take him for, I am sure your parents will wish you to be kind to him, and do all you can to help him on."

Many of the boys took the master's advice; but Nat Pilcher, and two or three of his particular friends still held out against Jem, and made his school hours as un-pleasant to him as they could.

One afternoon he was hurrying home from work, when a turn of the lane brought him suddenly on a group of children who were clustered round a fine old elm, and peering intently into its topmost branches.

"Oh do come here, and stop Nat Pilcher," said little Nancy, as she caught sight of Jem ; " he's up getting a bird's nest."

"But I can't hinder him," answered Jem, trying to keep steadily on.

"O yes, you can, you took the master's dog away from him the other day when he was teasing it. Don't let him get the poor birds," and Nancy pulled Jem into the little circle of gazers.

" Come down, and let the birds alone, Nat," said Jem, in the mildest tone of expostulation he could command ; "you know Mr. Bracy does not like us to touch them."

But Nat vouchsafed no reply, and the next minute Jem's coat was off, and branch after branch was cracking and swaying to and fro under his weight. He had just disappeared into the thick foliage that formed Nat's retreat, when Mr. Bracy came suddenly on the little group of school children, and comprehended at a glance what was going on.

" So you are bird's-nesting again," he said, angrily.

The children shrank back abashed, and the crashing of branches overhead suddenly ceased. The vicar looked up, but not being able to catch a glimpse of the offender, he asked who was in the tree.

" Please, sir, there's two of 'em," answered one of the boys, "Nat Pilcher and Jem Hazel."

" Jem Hazel !—I'm sorry for that, I didn't know he was a cruel boy."

"And he isn't indeed, sir," said Nancy; "he only got up to stop Nat."

"Ah, that was right! Well, come down, boys, both of you."

Jem obeyed instantly, but the command had to be repeated in a sterner tone before Nat thought fit to attend to it."

"So I have caught you at your old tricks again, Nat." said Mr. Bracy, as the two boys stood before him.

"I didn't mean, sir," began Nat, but looking round, he saw so many angry faces that he felt sure any clever invention of his would only meet with instant contradiction; so he wisely altered his tone, and said humbly, "Please, sir, I'm very sorry, and I'll never do it again."

"Very well, Nat. I never knew a cruel boy turn out good for anything yet, so I hope you'll to try correct yourself in time. Remember a little oftener who made the sparrows, and still feeds and cares for them, and that will make you less ready to injure them. Now, Jem, put on your coat, and come with me. How is it I haven't seen you in my garden this week?"

"We've been so busy haymaking, sir, that I couldn't be spared," answered Jem, as he walked on at Mr. Bracy's side. "It's vexed me a good deal, but I hope to be able to make it up next week."

"Well, there's no hurry about it; you've worked in such good earnest when you have been at it, Jem, that it can't come to much harm just yet. And how do you get on at school?"

"I hardly know, sir; sometimes I can't see that I'm making any progress at all."

"Ah, that's because you're too anxious about it, I expect. Keep steadily on, and results are sure to follow. But you don't look very hopeful about it, Jem."

"I get a good deal to vex me, sir, one way and another. There's some in the school, I know, who think I've no business to be there."

"Well, you must have as little as possible to do with them till they change their opinion. Have you done your work at the farm for to-day?"

"Yes, sir."

"Then you can help to nail up a little of my wall-fruit. Run home, and tell your mother you'll get your tea at the vicarage this evening."

"She's working at Hayburn, sir, and won't be back for a good bit yet. But I don't often trouble about tea. I'd sooner begin the trees at once, and get as much as I can done before dark."

However, as soon as the vicarage was reached, Jem was despatched into the kitchen, and regaled with a very substantial tea. Then he found what tools he needed, and went to his work in the garden. Miss Mary was already there, waiting, apparently, for his coming.

"Shan't we have a lot of peaches this year, Jem?"

"Yes, miss, there's a fine show on this tree."

"And papa says they are all to be kept till Edward comes home: that will be just about the time they're ripe."

"But I expect Master Edward won't care much about 'em, miss."

"Not about eating them, I dare say; but he loves

everything in the place, so we want to keep all the best fruit and flowers till he comes. What are you picking so carefully off that leaf, Jem ? "

" Only a beetle, miss."

" Then why don't you kill it ? John always kills everything he finds about the garden."

" But I don't think such things as them do any harm. I never saw one, that I know of, on a leaf before."

" Where do they live, then, and what do they get to eat ? "

" Well, I don't know, miss. I've seen 'em shining sometimes in the road, but I've never watched 'em long enough to see where they went to."

" Perhaps you might find out without taking the trouble," said the vicar, whose study-window was not far off from the peach-tree. " I'll lend you a book about insects, and, no doubt, you'll find your friend's likeness there, and some of his habits."

" Thank you, sir ; but I couldn't have thought such a thing as that had got into a book."

" But it has, Jem," said the vicar, as he stepped on to the lawn ; " and many other insects that you would think, perhaps, even less important. But here is the book, and you may read about them for yourself."

" But what's the use of Jem's learning about insects, papa ? " asked little Mary, who had no special love for study of any kind.

" Well, we shall see, my child," answered Mr. Bracy, thoughtfully ; and later in the evening, he took little Mary on his knee, and told her the story of a poor cobbler, who used to collect flowers and insects by the hedge sides as he wandered about to sell his wares, and whose name, years afterwards, ranked high in the annals of Christian missions.

"And will Jem be a great missionary?" asked Mary.

"Well, no! I hardly expect that; but he's a good boy, and anxious to learn, so I think we can't be doing wrong to help him on."

As the summer advanced, Jem's duties at the farm multiplied so rapidly, that he found very little time to devote to his own improvement. Some weeks he was not able to go to school at all, and then the care of the vicar's garden had to be left chiefly to his old servant.

"Here, Jem," said Mr. Bracy, as Jem made his appearance one sultry evening at the vicarage, "I think these trees want looking to. Are you very tender of earwigs?"

"No, sir, I always kill hurtful things."

"Then you'll find plenty to do here. John's eyes are not so good as they used to be, and I'm afraid if we leave the fruit to him, he'll let the earwigs get the first nibble at it. What do you think of the peaches now, Jem?"

"They look very fine, sir, nearly ready for Mr. Edward."

"Yes, and he'll not keep them waiting long. We shall have him home in a week or two, I expect."

There was to be a missionary meeting that evening at the next town, and, before he had been at work many minutes, Jem saw old John and two of the maid-servants pass out at a side gate. Shortly after the vicar crossed the lawn, hat in hand.

" I must leave you and Martha in charge this evening, Jem," he said ; " go in and get a good supper, my boy, when you've done your work."

" Thank you, sir."

Working in the vicarage garden was Jem's pleasantest pastime. He could take things leisurely there, and indulge his taste for beauty and order by looking at the trim walks, and the picturesque old house, especially that part of it, the study window, that shut in such stores of wonderful knowledge. Jem's musings were unusually cheerful that evening. Irregular as his attendance at school had necessarily been, his master had frequently expressed great satisfaction at his pro-gress, and his school-fellows, including even Nat Pilcher, were growing more friendly.

Later in the evening he had little Mary's company for a while, and there was no lack on either side of pleasant matters to talk about. The wonders Jem had discovered in his book of insects were discussed with great interest ; and then Mary told him the story of the great missionary.

" I wonder what his name was, Miss Mary," said Jem ; " do you know ? "

" No, but papa does ; he's got a book about him. Would you like to read it ? "

" Yes, if it isn't too nice to be handled."

" Oh, I don't expect it is. I'll ask papa about it to-morrow." And Jem went home that evening to give a last look at his book of insects before changing it for the life of the great missionary.

He was spared from work a little earlier than usual the next day, and set off at once to school. A group of boys were outside the gate, talking away with great earnestness, but they drew back, as Jem approached, and looked at him with unusual interest.

"I say," said Nat Pilcher, "was you working at Mr. Bracy's last night?"

"Yes," answered Jem; "what do you ask for?"

"Oh, nothing, only I wouldn't say anything about it if I was you."

"Why not?"

The boys looked at each other and laughed.

"Oh, of course, you don't know," said Nat, whose mirth had been loudest. "Never mind, perhaps you'll find out before long."

On entering the school all the children, and even the master, looked gravely at him, a reception that Jem did not at all like; however, he went quietly to his place, and got through his work as well as he could. Just before leaving the master put his hand kindly on his arm, and told him to look in again some time that evening, as he wanted to speak to him.

"Yes, sir," and Jem went slowly homewards, wondering what had happened. As he passed down the lane that skirted one side of the vicarage garden, he heard his name softly uttered, and saw his little friend, Miss Mary, at the open gate.

"Oh, do come here, Jem. Have you heard about it?"

" About what, Miss Mary ?"

" The peaches ; they're all gone ! Some one came last night and took them."

Jem was seized with a sudden fit of breathlessness, and sat down on the bank to recover himself, and think the matter over. When he had done both he asked Miss Mary if she knew who had taken them.

" No ; they say it was you, Jem, but I don't believe that."

" Who says I took them ? "

" Old John. You had only been gone a few minutes when he came home, and he thinks no one could have got in after that.' But never mind, come in, and tell papa you didn't take them."

" No, not now, Miss Mary, it wouldn't be any use. I'd rather wait." And Jem kept on again down the lane.

He had no heart to go home and tell his mother what had happened, so he wandered about until he thought Mr. Dunn would be expecting him.

By the time he got back to the school it was nearly dark. He went round, at first, to the master's room, but, seeing a bright light shining from the window he turned back to the empty school-room, and waited patiently there. After some time the master entered, and started back on seeing Jem.

" Why didn't you come into my room, Jem ?" he said ; " I'd almost given you up."

" Please, sir, I thought I'd rather stay here."

" I suppose you know what I want to speak to you about ?"

" Yes, sir."

"It's a bad business, Jem. Come here, I want to show you something that was found in one of the hedges close by this afternoon."

The master went to his desk and took a bundle from behind it. It was so loosely tied together that, as he threw it down, a portion of its contents—two large peaches—rolled out, and fell on the floor at Jem's feet. He picked them up quietly, and put them down on the desk.

"Do you know anything of this, Jem ?" asked the master, holding up a corner of the wrapper.

"Yes, sir, it's an old handkerchief of Master Edward's that Mr. Bracy gave me, with some other things, about a month ago."

"But you can't be sure of it's being yours. I dare say Mr. Bracy has given away a good many handkerchiefs just like it at different times."

"But I know this one, sir, because there's a piece out of the corner, and mother was going to cut off the whole side and hem it afresh; but how them peaches came to be in it I don't know any more than you do, sir. However, things look so black against me that I suppose it's no use for me to say so."

"I don't think there's any need, my boy. I have always seen you behave like a good honest lad, and I do not believe you guilty. Appearances are strong against you, but I do not believe appearances in this case."

"You're very kind, sir. I have tried indeed to get a good character, and it seems hard that this should come just as people were beginning to trust me a bit."

"Well, so it does, but you must be patient, and it

will all come out before long, I dare say. You are not the first, Jem, who has had to bear up, for a while, under a false accusation."

"Do you think, sir," asked Jem, his mind going back to an old trouble, "that it was so with—"

"With your father? No, Jem, I'm afraid not. The wrong was openly avowed there, and gloried in. But you mustn't trouble your head about that."

"I can't help it, sir, they're always bringing it up against me. Sometimes it seems as if it would be best for mother and me to leave the place altogether. We often talk of it."

"But I think that would be very foolish, because you would be leaving all your old friends. The Bible says, 'Commit thy way unto the Lord, and He will bring it to pass.' Can't you work on quietly, trusting in that promise, Jem?"

"I'll try to, sir, if you think it best. But there's Mr. Bracy—perhaps he'll never like to see me in his garden again."

"Yes, he will. I saw him this afternoon, and he told me he wished you to work there just as usual. Come, you must keep up a good heart, and try to do your best, as I believe you have done so far."

"Thank you, sir, for saying so," answered Jem, gratefully; and he took up his cap to go, but still lingered after wishing Mr. Dunn good-night.

"I shouldn't so much mind, sir," he said, at last, "if all this could be kept from mother. I'm afraid it'll almost break her heart."

"Why, can't she trust you, Jem, as I do?"

"O yes, sir, I've no fear about that. Only it will seem like the old trouble over again."

"No, it won't, Jem. The best thing you can do is to go straight home and tell her everything."

Jem did so, and found that the master was right. His mother listened to his story a little tremblingly at first, but when she had heard all she said cheerfully, "What a thing it is to have a good character, Jem. There isn't many boys in the school that the master and Mr. Bracy would have stood by as they have by you."

So the worst of his trouble being over, Jem thought he could face the rest, and bear it patiently, whatever came.

In the village there seemed but one opinion as to his guilt. "Like master like man," was the cry everywhere, the proverb being supposed to hold good just as well between father and son ; and whenever the affair of the stolen peaches was discussed the Pilchers' voices were the loudest in their condemnation. Nat, of course, again held himself disdainfully aloof from all intercourse with Jem ; but he condescended to take part occasionally in any proceedings that were going forward to annoy him. Other boys and girls grew shy of him again ; and little Nancy, much against her will, had to look out for a fresh champion for the poor birds, but, not succeeding in finding one, she could only stand by and cry while their nests were being rifled.

One evening, when Jem was busy in his garden, Nancy's little face peered suddenly in at the half-open gate.

"O Jem, I've come to tell you I'm so sorry I took

the peaches in to the master ; but I didn't know they were done up in your handkerchief."

" Never mind, you did quite right, Nancy. But how did you come to find them ? "

" Nat Pilcher sent me after his ball that he'd thrown over the hedge, and when I went round I saw the bundle lying close by it."

" And did he tell you to take it in to the master ? "

" Yes. We looked inside, and when we saw the peaches, Nat said the master ought to know, and he wanted Harry Bird to take 'em in to him ; but he wouldn't."

" Why couldn't he go himself ? "

" I don't know ;. perhaps he didn't like to any more than Harry."

" So then you took 'em ? " suggested Jem.

" Yes ; Nat said he'd give me one of the peaches if I'd go."

" But they weren't his to give."

" No, and so I didn't have it. But I took the peaches to the master, and told him where I'd found them."

" And how did it come out about the handkerchief, Nancy ? do you know ? "

" Yes, it was Harry Bird that told. When the master held it up in school, and asked if any of us knew who it belonged to, Harry said he thought it was yours. But he didn't want to say so, I could see, only Nat kept pushing him on."

" He must have looked at it pretty close to know it again," said Jem. " I'm sure I should have a hard job to say what any of his was like, or Nat's either."

" Yes, and the master wanted to know why Harry thought the handkerchief was yours, and he said because there was a bit out of the corner. Then the master asked how he'd found that out when he hadn't held the torn end up, and Harry looked very red, and didn't answer a word; but Nat said they'd both seen the handkerchief as I was taking it into school."

" So they had," said Jem. " Well, a bit out of a handkerchief is a thing one's likely to take notice of. I'd forgot that. But don't stand there, Nancy; come in and have a look at my garden."

" No, I mustn't, Jem, though I'd like to very much. How nice you keep it, and what pretty flowers you've got there !—white and pink and crimson."

"They're asters," said Jem. " Farmer Neal gave me the seeds, and now he says mine are finer than his. I suppose it's the care they get. If you wait a minute I'll pick you some."

" No, thank you, Jem, mother would be angry if she saw them. Good-night, I must run home now." And Jem being left to himself could not help wondering, as he groped in the dim light among his flowers, how it was that Nat Pilcher's ball had managed to find out the hiding-place of the stolen peaches.

For the next few days Jem did not see anything of little Nancy, either in the village or at school, and at last he ventured to ask her elder sister what had become of her.

" She's at home," was the short answer.

" But why doesn't she come to school? Isn't she well ? "

" I don't know, I'm sure. She keeps pretty quiet in bed, so I expect she's having a nice easy time of it."

Jem did not feel quite satisfied about that ; and the next evening he gathered a bunch of his prettiest asters, and went down to the Prices' cottage.

Sarah Price, Nancy's mother, was not by any means a gentle-spirited woman. She was busy ironing, when Jem's footsteps outside her door made her suddenly look up, and she gave him anything but a pleasant glance of recognition.

" Well, Jem Hazel, and what do you want ? "

" Why, I heard Nancy wasn't well, and so I thought she might like some flowers."

" And if she did there's no need to go further for 'em than our own garden," and Sarah went on briskly with her ironing.

But Jem did not cut his best flowers every day in the week, and had no idea of being put off so easily. Looking up a minute or two after, Sarah saw that he was still standing in the doorway.

" You seem to have more time than you know what to do with," she said crossly.

" No, I haven't ; but I want Nancy to get these flowers, because I know she'll like 'em."

" Well, if you're so bent on it you may go in there," and Sarah nodded towards an inner door. " But mind you're pretty quiet, for I don't want her woke up if she's asleep."

Jem opened the door softly, and looked into the room beyond. Little Nancy was lying on a bed at the further end, dreamily watching the delicate sprays of some creeping plants that were moving gently to and fro outside the open window. As he used less caution in his movements on seeing she was awake, Nancy looked up, and smiled brightly at the sight of Jem and his flowers:

" O Jem ! does mother know you've brought 'em ?"

" Yes, she said I might come in and give 'em to you."

Nancy took the flowers, and spread them out on the neat white coverlet of her little bed. Then she set to work to arrange them, a business that had to be repeated three or four times before she was satisfied, and consented to their being consigned to the jug of water Jem had fetched for them. It seemed hard work to part with them; but when they were placed on the window-sill, where the creeping plant outside formed a sober green back-ground, they looked so bright that Nancy could do nothing for some time but lie quite still and admire them.

" They're just what I wanted, Jem," she said; " I got so tired of only seeing the green ; and now I seem to have all sorts of colours to look at."

" Yes, it's dull work lying here, I expect," said Jem.

He was standing at the foot of the bed in some perplexity. It was his first visit to a sick-room, and he did not quite know how to get through it. Going away directly his flowers were delivered seemed unkind, for Nancy must sadly want companionship; but he was at a loss to know what he should do to amuse her if he stayed. Out at the hedge sides he would have been in no difficulty; but nothing likely to afford entertainment was to be seen in that bare room ; and conversation was by no means Jem's *forte.*

" I must bring you a story-book from school, Nancy," he said, at last.

" O no, thank you, Jem, I couldn't read it because I get so soon tired ; and Martha wouldn't."

" Then suppose I do ; I could spare half an hour or so of an evening."

" But that's your time for learning, Jem."

" O never mind ; I can manage somehow. Besides, you're not going to be ill long."

" I hope not, it's so much trouble for mother. Would you mind staying a little while now, Jem ? "

" No, not a bit. But we haven't got any book."

" O yes, we have ; I like Bible stories best," and Nancy drew her little school Bible from beneath her pillow. Jem took the book, and sat down at the bedside, but was at a loss to know where to begin. Nancy, however, selected the portions she wished to hear, and helped Jem to find them. They were, Jesus receiving little children, and the healing of Jairus's daughter. When he had finished he asked if he should read any more, but Nancy said she would rather talk over what she had heard, and a conversation followed in which she took by far the largest share. The extent of her Bible knowledge, and her readiness at imparting it, were a great marvel to Jem, who would have found it a difficult matter to put into words the result of any of his own quiet musings.

" I wonder how you got to know so much, Nancy ? " he said.

" Oh, I don't know much, Jem. But when I used to stay in the town with grandmother, she sent me to Sunday-school there, and then Miss Anstey taught me— a nice kind lady, who made everything so plain. Sometimes she used to come to see grandmother, and read to her, and that was how I came to know more about the Bible."

" I wish we'd one or two such teachers here," said Jem.

" So do I," said Nancy. "That's why I love the Bible and Martha doesn't. She never heard Miss Anstey read it, and talk about it. How I should like to see her now! But grandmother told me she was married, and going to teach poor children a long way off."

That made Jem think of some missionary scheme of his own, originated by his last talk with Miss Mary in the vicarage garden; and he communicated it with much hesitation to Nancy.

" You'll have a deal to learn, Jem, before then," was Nancy's grave remark.

" Yes." The consciousness of that and of his own dull powers was often a heavy weight on Jem's mind. He sat for some time looking, as Nancy had done, at the swaying foliage at the window. Then he wished her good-night, and went out. Sarah Price was still busy with her irons as he passed through, but she stopped for a moment to ask how his mother was—an attention that more than atoned, in Jem's estimation, for the ungracious reception she had given him.

On his road homeward a fly, laden with luggage,

rattled past Jem, and kept on up the lane at a rapid pace. Any vehicle lighter than a waggon was a sufficiently novel sight in that quiet village to attract attention, and he looked after the fly with wondering eyes till it turned the corner of the lane. Following on at his own leisurely pace, he came suddenly upon it again, drawn up at the side gate of the vicarage. Old John was dragging the luggage from the top, and Mr. Bracy and another gentleman were standing inside the shrubbery. Not having been at the vicarage since the affair of the peaches, Jem tried to pass on unperceived, but a shout from Mr. Bracy obliged him to turn back.

" Come here, Jem, and help in with these things."

Jem obeyed, and on passing out again he ventured to look more steadily at the strange gentleman.

" Well," said the vicar, " don't you know him ? "

" Yes, sir, it's Mr. Edward."

But Jem's answer was only a guess, for it was difficult to identify that tall, grave-looking young man with the merry youth who had left the vicarage little more than a year before.

A fresh surprise awaited Jem on the following Sunday. As he entered his class he saw that the deaf old farmer, who had held the post of teacher there for years, was gone, and Mr. Edward installed in his place. All went on pretty much as usual, till the hymns and Bible verses were repeated, and then a sharp catechising followed, instead of the old wearisome repetition. Nat Pilcher, and one or two quick-witted boys, acquitted themselves very fairly, but Jem blundered sadly, and drew on himself more than once grave looks of disapproval. Still he bore them cheerfully, thinking he could not pay too dearly for the privilege of being under such a teacher; and never before, since he first formed that scheme of far-off enterprise, had his hopes of success been so high. But they were very near being clouded again that afternoon. Two or three elder boys entered the class before the lesson began, and Jem with another boy of his own age were being moved out of it to make room for the fresh comers, when Mr. Bracy, who happened to be passing down the school at the moment, promptly interfered.

"No, I can't have that boy moved down, Edward," said he; "there's more in him than you think for."

Jem resumed his place, and finding his slowness of thought and utterance more patiently borne, he took courage, and did no discredit to Mr. Bracy's kind commendation.

Little Nancy listened with great interest to Jem's report of the school doings, her only regret being that the boon of a good teacher was not extended to Martha's class as well. But the poor child was getting rapidly worse, and was soon too ill to receive even Jem's quiet visits. A slow fever, prevalent in some parts of the village towards the close of the year, was beginning its fatal work earlier than usual that autumn; and before Nancy Price was out of danger, several other cases had occurred. Mr. Bracy and his son paid great attention to the sick, who were chiefly children—little things who found it weary work to lie still in bed while the bright sun was shining out of doors—and before long, without any intention on his part of putting himself forward, Jem was added to the little band of kindly visitants. Meeting a neighbour of the Prices one evening, as he was returning from work, she asked him if he would go in and read to her Jane as he had to little Nancy. Jem readily consented, and as the sickness spread, the demands for his services rapidly increased. Everywhere, though he had very little to say, his quiet evening visits were eagerly looked for by the sick children. Sometimes he read books to them from the school library, but often he found Bible stories more eagerly received, and even when the little sufferers were too ill to listen to anything, they were sure to brighten up at the sight of his kind sympathizing looks. The time he had looked forward to for self-improvement at home was sadly broken into, but he was a patient lad, and, as every one said the illness could not last long, he was quite ready to wait, and do his own work when it was over.

But a warm hazy October spread the fever to the higher parts of the village. Little Mary Bracy was attacked, but she soon recovered, and was running about again wherever it was safe for her to venture. Even the Pilchers, though their cottage was quite out of the village, were severely visited. One of their children was the first among the fever-stricken sufferers to die, and a few days after, Nat and two of his younger brothers were lying ill together. Jem did not forget their cottage in his rounds, but he was never encouraged to go beyond the door-way. Nat always sat up on the defensive at the sight of his old schoolmate, as though

H

he had come with some hostile intent, and stoutly maintained that he was all right, and didn't want any one
to come prying round after him. Still Jem persevered,
hoping some day to meet with a better reception. But
it never came; and before long Nat was able to leave
his bed altogether, and extended his jealous guard of
his own domain even beyond the doorway.

Round the Prices' cottage, which was in the lowest
part of the village, the cases of sickness were more
numerous than elsewhere; and after the bell had tolled
for little Tom Pilcher, it was often heard again booming
out in the quiet autumn air. Still the children, who
were able to run about, played as merrily in the lanes
as they used to before sickness and death settled down
among them. Sometimes when Jem went to pay his
evening visit to Nancy he found her sister Martha leading some noisy game out of doors—a sure sign, he soon
discovered, that she was left in charge of the cottage,
and its little sick inmate. Then Nancy would rouse
up with a bright smile on seeing him, and Jem, unless
he had very pressing calls elsewhere, would stay with
her until her mother came home, or Martha's game was
finished.

One evening he found her lying half asleep, with her
face turned towards the open window. There were no
flowers on the sill, and the creeping plant outside was
stripped of its green foliage, but more beautiful than
either, perhaps, in Nancy's dreamy eyes was the evening
star, gleaming down with its soft clear radiance. Jem
stood for a minute looking at her, and then, thinking
the room seemed dull, he went back to brighten up the

kitchen fire with a handful of wood. Nancy heard him moving about, and called out to know who was there.

"It's me," said Jem, reappearing at her open door; "I'm trying to get the fire up, and let a bit of light in here."

"O no, I don't want any. The light shuts the stars out, and I'd rather see them. Look at that bright one, Jem, right opposite, and the little one higher up. I've been watching them come out, and wondering about them."

"About the stars?"

"Yes; I think Miss Anstey said something about them once, and I have been trying to recollect what it was, but perhaps I shall hear again soon."

"Why, is she coming back?"

"Not that I know of, Jem; I wasn't thinking about that."

Jem looked at Nancy for a few moments in silence, then some change in her looks suggested a clue to her meaning.

"But you're getting better, Nancy; everybody says so."

"Yes, I know they do."

"And they must be right."

Nancy made no answer. She was either getting drowsy again, or felt indisposed to argue the point with him; so he sat quietly by her till her mother came in, bringing the truant Martha.

A little way up the lane Jem met the vicar, coming out of a cottage gate.

" Well, Jem," he said, kindly, " I think it's time you
and I were at home."

" Yes, sir.   Is any one ill in there ? " and Jem nodded
towards the gate Mr. Bracy had just closed behind
him.

" Yes, Harry Bird—a bad case I'm afraid ; the poor
boy seems very low."

" And he has no mother to nurse him, sir."

" No, that makes it worse for him.   Poor Jane Bird !
her death was a sad loss to her children.   They have
never seemed to go right since."

" I think Harry has been led on by others to do
wrong, sir."

" Very likely !   The sure result of choosing bad
companions.   But there's old dame Bright at her door ;
so I'll just look in and see how her grand-daughter's
getting on."

Mr. Bracy passed into the cottage, and Jem plodded
homewards wondering with grave concern how Harry
was to get through his illness with no one to nurse
him.

The question was discussed over supper with his
mother that night, and when the meal was finished he
was not surprised to see her putting on her bonnet and
shawl.

" I'll just go round and see he's comfortable for the
night, Jem," she said.   " You can leave the door on the
latch for me."

Jem cleared away the supper things, but not feeling
disposed to go to bed, he took down a book, and sat
reading till his mother came back.   She brought a good

account of Harry. He was sleeping quietly, and she had left his medicine at his side, and told one of the younger children what was to be done when he awoke.

Jem's first visit the next evening was to Harry Bird. He was half asleep when Jem entered the room, but he soon roused up sufficiently to show as much dislike to his quiet presence as Nat Pilcher had done.

" Well, I thought you'd like to see me," said Jem ; "anything's better than being alone."

" No, it isn't," murmured Harry from beneath the bedclothes. " I don't want to see you nor any one."

Jem stood considering this strange state of affairs for a minute with a puzzled face. Then suddenly thinking that Harry's dislike to see him might be connected in some way with his giving information respecting the ownership of the unlucky handkerchief in which the peaches were tied up, he told him that if that were the case he was not to trouble himself any more about it.

"About what ? " said Harry, starting up. "What handkerchief ? "

" Why, the one with the corner out that you told the master was mine."

" I shouldn't have done it if it hadn't been for Nat."

"Well, it doesn't matter now. Mr. Bracy didn't believe I stole his peaches, though things did look so black against me."

" Didn't he ? Who does he think took 'em, then ? "

" I don't know. Here, never mind about that now, Harry; I've brought you something nice from the vicarage, and Mr. Bracy says you're to send up Susan for anything you fancy."

Jem uncovered a nice plate of jelly, but Harry pushed it away, and turned his face again out of sight.

" Well, I'll leave it here," said Jem, putting the plate down at Harry's side, " and you'll have mother round to see you presently."

" No, I don't want her. Tell her not to come."

But Jem did not deliver the message; and when his mother went round, a little later, to see Harry, she thought him so much worse that she remained with him a great part of the night.

Jem's visit to little Nancy that evening was a very sad one. She was too ill to be disturbed, and he could only look at her for a minute through the open door of her room, and then steal quietly away. It was the last time he saw her. The next afternoon Martha came sobbing to school, and Jem learnt that Nancy had passed away in the night.

The lanes were very quiet that evening, as Jem plodded wearily along them. Nancy had been a great favourite in the village, and for a few days the children gave up their noisy games, and got together in little groups to talk about their lost playmate. Poor Martha sorrowed with a troubled conscience, and showed her contrition for her past neglect of Nancy by keeping close in her little room now that care and watchfulness were no longer needed there.

Jem did not care to go and see Harry Bird again

very soon. Nancy's death had cast him down a good deal, and he had not heart to present himself where he knew he should not be welcome. But about a week after, as he was leaving school, one of the children went up to him, and told him Harry Bird wanted to see him.

"And what for, I should like to know?" said Nat Pilcher, who had got out that day for the first time, and was sunning himself on a bank outside the school-gate. "Suppose I go, I'm tired of sitting here, and one'll do as well as another."

Jem wavered for a moment. Nat had been a great ally of Harry's, and perhaps he would like to see him best; however his steady habit of doing simply what he was told, induced Jem finally to go himself, and he set off down the lane at once without heeding Nat's re-monstrances.

The bell was tolling as Jem passed through the village. Little Nancy was to be buried that afternoon, and as stroke after stroke pealed out he had to draw his hand very often across his eyes. A short distance from the churchyard he met the funeral procession—a little coffin, carried by four young bearers, dressed in white, and half-a-dozen mourners behind. He took off his cap and stood on one side as it passed; then having watched it up the steep hill-side to the church gates, where Mr. Bracy was waiting to receive it, he kept on sorrowfully to the Birds' cottage.

He found Harry still in bed, and looking wretchedly ill. He started up as Jem entered his room, and stared at him with such a scared expression in his face that

Jem began to fear the fever was getting to some very alarming height.

"Come, it's only me, Harry," said Jem, "there's nothing to be afraid of."

"I know that," returned Harry, sullenly; "who said there was?"

"Why you—at least you look like it."

"And so would you if you had been lying here all this long while, as I have. Oh, there it goes again, Jem! Isn't it dreadful to hear it!"

"What, the bell? why that's done! It's only the clock you hear striking. But you've never let the bell frighten you, surely?"

"I don't know. It's a dreadful thing to be left to die here all alone!"

"But you're not going to die, I hope. Mother said you were better yesterday."

"I don't feel like it."

"And then you needn't have been alone if you hadn't wished it. I'd have been down often to see you, and others too. There was Nat Pilcher wanting to come off just now instead of me."

"Did he? I know what that was for. He was afraid I should tell, and I will; I can't bear it any longer. It's been dreadful to have your mother about me all this week, and to see the nice things they sent me from the vicarage. But I never touched 'em, I couldn't; they'd have choked me! Neddy and Susan eat 'em all."

Jem looked at his old schoolmate for a moment in great perplexity. Then he went to a pitcher of water that was standing near, poured some in his hands, and said soothingly—

"Come lie down, Harry, and I'll bathe your head a bit."

"No, it doesn't want any bathing. What's that ı.oise down-stairs, Jem? Go and see, and if it's Nat don't let him come in!"

But it was only Neddy Bird, with his slate and book-bag, trying hard to reach the latch. Jem let the child in, and then went back to Harry, who was looking a little pacified.

"I don't want to see Nat any more," he said; "he's a bad boy, and has often led me on to do wicked things. I wish I'd minded what mother told me, and never had anything to do with him."

"Well, it would have been better, Harry. Mr. Bracy was saying the other day that you hadn't been going on so well lately."

"Did he? What made him say that? Had—had he found out anything fresh?"

"Not that I know of; but I dare say he's heard how often you've played truant at school."

Harry kept quite still for a minute or two, with closed eyes. Then he said in a low voice, "Jem, I can't bear it any longer, so it shall all come out. You recollect the peaches?"

Of course Jem did; and he asked Harry, with a heightened colour, if he knew anything about them.

"Yes, it was Nat and me that took 'em."

"And then tried to put it on me! O Harry, how could you!"

"No, that was Nat's doing. After you were gone that night we got into Mr. Bracy's garden, just to have a peach or two. We didn't intend to take more, at least I didn't, but when Nat once began eating there was no stopping him. O dear, how frightened I was! I thought Mr. Bracy or old John would be down upon us every minute."

"But about the handkerchief," said Jem, eagerly; "how did you get that?"

"I found it as I was creeping round the wall, in coming out again. You'd dropp'd it, I suppose, while you were at your work that evening, but I threw it over to Nat, thinking it was his."

"And how did the peaches come to be in it? Did you go back and fill it?"

"No, at least I didn't. I never saw the handkerchief again till Nancy Price had hold of it, and then Nat told me it was yours, and that if I didn't say so when the master asked who it belonged to, he'd go straight up to him and let out all we'd done. O Jem, I've never had a minute's peace since for thinking of it. If Mr. Bracy was to find it out he'd never forgive me!"

"You mustn't let it come to that," said Jem; "you must tell him."

"Tell him!" repeated Harry, looking whiter than ever." I couldn't, Jem; I should die of fright."

"No, you wouldn't. You'll be better when it's over, and you've asked Mr. Bracy to forgive you."

"Yes, if I only felt sure he would! O Jem, you don't know what I've gone through, lying here all by myself at night, and feeling every minute that I was getting worse, and going to die. And death's so dreadful!"

"Not always," and Jem told Harry of the peace little Nancy had at the last, and her joy at the thought that all the things her teacher had told her—so difficult in her illness to remember and understand—were going to be made plain to her.

"Oh! she hadn't anything on her mind," said Harry, turning uneasily on his bed. "Jem, will you tell Mr. Bracy?"

"No, I think it would come better from you, and Mr. Bracy will be more likely to look it over if you speak up yourself."

"Well, when I get better I'll try."

"If you wait for that you'll never do it."

"Why, ain't I going to get well?"

"No, not till you've got this load off your mind. Come, I'll tell Mr. Bracy you want to see him the next time he's round this way, and then he'll be prepared for something."

Harry looked so white and faint at the bare idea of his confession being so near, that Jem was a little alarmed, and made him swallow some beef-tea that had been standing untasted by his side all day. That seemed to revive him a good deal, so Jem told him, as he wished him good-night, that he thought he might as well go round to Mr. Bracy at once.

"O no, Jem, pray don't; let's leave it till to-morrow."

"But what's the good of waiting?"

" I don't know. Well, you won't leave it all for me, will you? Just put in a word first."

Jem promised to do that, and then hurried away, for fear Harry's courage should fail again. As he was passing through the churchyard he saw Mr. Bracy and the old clerk leisurely coming down one of the paths. Some business had detained them at the church after little Nancy's funeral was over. Jem waited at the gate till the vicar had passed through it, and then told his errand.

" Wants to see me?" said Mr. Bracy, looking a little alarmed. " I hope he's not worse."

" No, sir; I think it's only being uneasy in his mind, and not taking what he ought to, that's brought him so low."

" Uneasy! What about, Jem?"

" Well, that's what he's got to tell you, sir. And please, sir, as he's very sorry, perhaps you won't be hard on him."

" Am I ever hard on any one, Jem?"

" No, sir, you ain't indeed. I oughtn't to have said that."

" Well, never mind; I'll see Harry before I go home. And Jem, come round to me this evening; there's something I want to speak to you about."

" Yes, sir."

Jem went home, and gave his mother, over tea, the substance of Harry Bird's confession. She was very glad at having Jem cleared, but felt a good deal for the motherless boy, who had shown more weakness than viciousness in the whole affair. Directly after tea she hurried away to see to Harry's wants, as she had done every evening during his illness; and a little later Jem went round to the vicarage.

The lamp was lit in Mr. Bracy's study by the time Jem reached it; so, thinking the vicar was engaged, he busied himself at a bed near the open French window till he was seen and called in.

"I suppose you know what Harry had to tell me, Jem?" said Mr. Bracy.

"Yes, sir—how he and Nat took the peaches. I'm glad the truth has come out at last."

"So am I, though I never had any suspicion against you, as you know."

"No, sir; you and the master were very good to me through it all."

"As we had every reason to be, Jem. You have always shown yourself a truthful, honest lad to us both, and it would have been hard if your good character had not borne witness in your favour. Besides, we were tolerably sure of the real culprits."

"Were you, sir?" said Jem, in surprise.

"Yes. Nat, I am sorry to say, has been concerned in such wrong-doings before, and tried to put the blame of them on to others. And Harry has seemed a good deal under his influence lately."

"I hope you won't think very ill of him for what he's done, sir. A bad boy wouldn't have had it on his mind so afterwards."

"No; I trust this will be a warning to him to keep out of bad company for the future. I'll see if Mr. Edward can take him into his class, and try to make something of him. And now, Jem, you shall hear what I wanted to speak to you about. You know the lodge at the Woodlands ?"

" Yes, sir ; I've often been there when Master Hart was alive."

" Well, his widow seems to be going to live with a married daughter, so the place will soon want a new tenant. Would you like to have it ?"

" Yes, sir; but we should be the last Squire Conyton would give it to."

" A year ago you certainly would, Jem ; but things are changed with you now. Mr. Conyton was asking me to recommend a new tenant for his lodge last night, and he made no objection when I mentioned your mother. It will be a nice home for her, Jem."

" It will indeed, sir," answered Jem, looking flushed and eager. " It was very kind of you to think of su."

" Well, I must not take all the credit of that, for I found your master, Farmer Neal, had been beforehand with me. So now you must talk the matter over with your mother, and she had better see Mr. Conyton about it some time to-morrow."

" Yes, sir. It'll be the best news I've ever had to take her."

Jem kept his position a little longer in front of Mr. Bracy, turning his cap uneasily round. He was greatly afraid that he had not expressed his gratitude as he ought ; but the slowness of speech that was sure to come over him at inopportune moments kept him silent. Mr. Bracy understood his difficulty, and wished him good-night with a kind smile.

"And don't forget my garden, Jem; I can't lose your services there."

"No, sir." And Jem left the study to carry his good news to his mother—the best, as he said, that he had ever had to take her.

"Take away the dross from the silver, and there shall come
forth a vessel for the finer."—PROV. xxv. 4.

"O JOHN! how could you make such a litter?"
said Ellen Foster, as she stood, with a dismayed
countenance, at the open door of a small apartment,
which served alternately as dining-room and study, but
which looked, just then, quite unfit to be put to any
orderly household purpose.

"Why, what's the matter? it's only my work,"
answered John, without lifting his eyes from his
Virgil.

"Do you call bits of paper and caricatures work,
and all this rubbish out of Harry's playbox?"

"Oh! the playbox is his affair.—I say, Harry, come
here and clear up your traps."

But Harry, who was whistling just outside the
window, vouchsafed no reply.

"There, it's no use making a bother," continued
John. "If Mary comes in before I've done this bit
of translation, I'll soon put everything straight."

Mary was the only servant belonging to the little
household, and at one o'clock it was her duty to put
the study through its transformation; and, as she had
no time to attend to anybody's work but her own,

books and papers were expected to be cleared away before the appearance of the dinner-cloth.

"But papa's orders are that the room is to be cleared at half-past twelve," said Ellen, "and it's after that now."

"Well, he did not tell me anything about it, so I may as well do a bit more work," and John stretched across the table for a huge dictionary; but it was arrested midway by Ellen, who said sharply, that if he did not mean to put away his things, she should do it herself.

"Oh, very well," replied John, "only let me get off first;" and tucking both Virgil and lexicon under his arm, he scrambled through the open window into the garden.

Ellen looked after him with a heavy sigh, and then stooped down to pick up the shreds of paper and boy's litter that strewed the ground. Before she had half finished, Mary came bustling in, and put her tray down on the side table.

"I am sorry the room is not ready yet," said Ellen. "But you need not wait—I'll call you as soon as I have put everything away."

Mary went out again, and the next minute Ellen heard the kitchen clock strike one. She jumped up, knowing that the next sound would probably be her papa's footstep in the passage. He was very punctual, especially on Saturday, when he always liked a long afternoon to finish his Sunday preparation. It was hopeless to think of arranging John's papers into any kind of order, so she gathered them all up in a heap,

I

and then found that an ink-bottle hidden underneath
was upset, and its contents flowing in a long stream
over the table-cloth.   This sight was the crowning
point of her vexation, and she burst into a passionate
fit of sobbing.   The next minute Mr. Foster's heavy
step crossed the passage, but Ellen did not look up
until his hand was pressed on her shoulder.

" Ellen, my child, what is the matter ? "

The papers had fallen from Ellen's grasp again, and
buried all signs of the disaster that had befallen the
table-cloth.

"The boys are so tiresome, papa, and don't mind
what I—what you say."

" Which of us has been disobeyed, Nelly ? " asked
Mr. Foster, smiling.

" O papa, I didn't mean that.   But you know you
said the room was always to be cleared at half-past
twelve, and John wouldn't give up in proper time, and
put away his things."

" He hasn't been back with us long, Nelly, and
perhaps does not know our rules yet.   Besides, if I
give orders, you must leave me to see them carried out.
You will find your own burden, my child, quite as much
as you can bear."

" And I haven't told you all yet, papa.   Hurrying to
got the table cleared, I upset the ink.   It was so hidden
under John's papers, that I didn't see it."

" Where are the boys ? '

" In the garden, papa."

Mr. Foster called them both in, and told them to put
away their things.   While they were getting through

their work he sat watching them with such sad weary eyes, that Ellen felt very sorry for having troubled him with her little vexations. Some few months before, when he had told her, one day, with a trembling voice, that she would have to be his little housekeeper for the future, she had determined to make home matters very smooth to him ; but somehow it had happened that she had never succeeded for one whole day in carrying out her resolve.

The dinner was ready at last, and the family, with the addition of Lenny, a bright little fellow of four, sat down to table. No one seemed disposed to talk, for Mr. Foster was tired with his morning's work in the village, and Ellen and the two elder boys looked rather uncomfortable. As soon as it was over, Mr. Foster rose and said to John,

" I suppose you mean to take a half-holiday this afternoon ? "

" Yes, papa, the Carrysfords want me to go out with them."

" And you, Harry ? "

" I should like to go too, papa ; only—"

Ellen looked sharply at Harry, but said nothing.

" Very well, my boy, I don't know anything to prevent it," and Mr. Foster began arranging the papers at his writing-table, a proceeding that on Saturday afternoon was always understood to be the signal for the children to leave the room. John and Harry dashed off in high glee, and Ellen followed more slowly with little Lenny.

When the tea hour came round, the boys had not

returned, but no one thought of altering any household arrangement to suit their convenience ; so Lenny was perched on his high chair, and Ellen carried a cup of tea round to her papa, who was still sitting at his own table. A minute or two after he took the empty cup back, and sat down at her side, saying his work was nearly finished, and so he should take the rest of his tea in comfort.

"How is this, Nelly ?" he said, as he looked at his little daughter. "Tears again ! what's the matter ?"

"It was my afternoon for practising at the church, papa, and I haven't been able to do it."

"Why ? Have you been so busy ?"

"No, papa, but you never like me to go alone, and Harry has been out ever since dinner."

"Oh, he quite forgot the practice, I dare say. Why didn't you remind him of it ?"

"I thought he ought to have remembered it himself."

"Well, so he ought ; but you see I was equally forgetful, or I should not have let him go off with John."

"But you have so much to think of, papa."

"So has Harry, no doubt. Perhaps his affairs are quite as engrossing in their way. You should have reminded him of his engagement with you when he asked to go out with John."

"But I don't think he quite forgot it, papa, for I saw him hesitate."

"Then a word from you would probably have decided the matter at once, for I have never seen him make any difficulty about going with you to the church. However, we shall have a couple of hours yet before sunset,

Page 133.

so that you can still get through your practice if Harry is not too late."

" But the afternoon is my time, papa. Harry knows that."

" *Your* time, Nelly ? is there only one to be considered in the arrangement ?"

" No, papa, two," answered Ellen, blushing.

" Then I think Harry's convenience ought to be studied a little as well as yours."

" Yes, but he has nothing to do but to amuse himself after lessons are over, and I have so much ; and you have told us that it is always best to have fixed times for doing things."

" Yes, if we can see them broken into occasionally without being put out. But now, if Harry is not home in half an hour, Nelly, you may put on your hat, and I will go round to the church with you."

" Oh thank you, papa. But are you sure you can spare the time ?"

" Yes, my work is nearly finished. Besides, if needful, I can sit up a little later to-night."

Greatly to Ellen's satisfaction the half-hour passed without anything being seen of Master Harry ; and then she put her music book under her arm, and set out with Mr. Foster for her hour's practice at the church.

They had not far to go. A little side gate of the vicarage garden opened at once into the churchyard, and then a narrow path bordered on either side with grassy mounds led up to the church. It was a small plain building, but too ancient to be altogether uninteresting. On two sides the walls were nearly covered with ivy, and it had a wide picturesque porch, into which Ellen was very fond of carrying books or work on sunny afternoons. Inside, the aspect of the church was less inviting. The stones were in many places broken and uneven, and the walls bare, and instead of pews, rows of time-worn benches were ranged on either side. Beyond the benches, and near the reading-desk, was the harmonium, which had originally been bought for Mrs. Foster, when she came to reside in the quiet vicarage close by; but for some time Ellen had had to take her place at the little instrument Sunday after Sunday, and go through the old psalm and hymn tunes that her mother used to play.

Mr. Foster looked very sad as the first notes of the harmonium struck on his ear that evening; then he took a book from his pocket, and sat on one of the old benches reading while Ellen practised.

She found her occupation so pleasant that it was prolonged far beyond the hour, and it was growing dark when she closed her instrument, and told her father she was ready to go.

" Don't you think I'm improving, papa?" she asked, as they crossed the churchyard again.

" In your playing, Nelly?"

" Yes, papa," and Ellen raised her eyes to her father's face, but they fell instantly, and she looked flushed and uncomfortable.

" I know you think that I have been in fault twice to-day, papa," she said, after a minute's hesitation, " but I cannot help being vexed when things are going wrong."

"What do you mean by going wrong?"

"Well, happening so as to upset one's plans. I had intended to be so punctual with your dinner to-day, when John and Harry prevented it by not having cleared away their things in proper time; and then you know about the practice."

"Yes. And do you always mean to let these trifles put you out of patience?"

"I don't know, papa—not when I am a grown woman, perhaps."

"And in the meantime, Nelly, what am I to do? You know I like a quiet household above all things."

"O yes, papa, and I have tried so hard to make everything pleasant for you."

"But not in the best possible way. I would rather you should give me my dinner a little behind its time, or lose your practice, than let me see you look cross and unhappy. Besides, you must not mistake the real end of trouble. Do you know why it is sent?"

"Trouble! O yes, papa, to make us better."

"I see you are thinking of great afflictions, Nelly. But, if we know them to be sent to improve us, is it reasonable to conclude that small vexations—the little thorns that spring up under our feet at every step—are only intended to put us out of temper?"

"O no, papa, of course not."

They were passing through the gate then that led into the vicarage garden, and on the other side they found Master Lenny doing sad mischief to one of the flower borders. Mr. Foster took him up in his arms, and, carrying him into the house, gave him into Mary's custody to be put to bed.

" Have the boys come in yet ?" he asked.

" No, sir—Mr. Carrysford has just sent round to say they wouldn't be back till after supper."

Ellen put away her hat and music-book up-stairs, and then, going softly into the dining-room, saw her father sitting alone in the twilight.

" Shall I bring your lamp, papa ?" she asked.

" Not yet ; reading in the dim old church has made me dreamy and idle. Come here and bear me company."

Ellen gladly obeyed, and drew a stool to her father's side.

" And now you may bring me the little drawer on the left side of my writing-table."

The drawer was brought, and Mr. Foster took from it something that looked like a coarse rough stone.

" You have seen this before, Nelly," he said, " and so will be able to tell what it is."

" Yes—an ore of some kind, papa."

" Of silver. Do you see any resemblance between it and this bright shilling ?"

" No, papa, but I know that there was one once."

" And that the shilling has undergone some transforming process since. Can you tell me what it was ?"

" I think I can, papa. The ore was placed in some vessel over a hot fire, and the lighter parts, or dross, that rose to the surface as they melted, skimmed off, till nothing but the pure metal remained behind."

" Do you know how the refiner ascertained when

the metal at the bottom of the vessel was sufficiently pure ?"

" No, papa."

" He watched it patiently, removing every coarse particle as it arose, till at last on the bright smooth surface he saw his own image clearly reflected."

" O yes, papa, I had forgotten that."

" Try to remember it then for the future, Nelly. Do you know of whom it is said, ' He shall sit as a refiner and purifier of silver ? ' "

" Yes, papa, of the Lord Jesus ; and by the silver is meant His people."

" Can you tell me some of the means He uses to refine, or make them holy ? "

" Yes ; trouble is one, papa."

" Then how ought we to take it ? "

" Very patiently."   And Ellen hung down her head.

" Yes ; not only the great affliction that may be coming very slowly towards you or me, Nelly, but the small troubles that assail us in our daily path, knowing that the end of them all is to fit us to bear some dim likeness to our great Lord and Teacher.   Suppose I give you this piece of ore as a reminder of what we have been talking about to-night ? "

" Thank you, papa ;   I will never forget to look at it when any little trouble seems likely to put me out again."

Ellen put the piece of ore in her pocket, and then, at her father's request, lit the lamp.

" I must have a very quiet hour now," he said ; " but you can stay here with your book or work if you like."

Ellen gladly availed herself of the permission, and sat reading in silence till her father's work was finished.

She had no more quiet evenings with Mr. Foster for some time after that. Instead of going on excursions with the Carrysfords every day, as he had done during the first part of his holiday, John now took it into his head to begin an important course of reading, and remain pertinaciously at home. Never was there such an unmanageable student before ! He found it necessary to have so many books and papers about, and to vary his mental labour with such frequent romps with Harry and Lenny, that it was impossible to keep a single corner of the dining-room tidy for ten minutes together. Ellen, who thought, and very correctly, that two things could not be done well at the same time, was shocked to see work and play going on together; but then, as John was in the midst of his Midsummer holidays, he probably fancied that great credit was due to him for making any pretence to work at all. Ellen and Harry still studied at home, but it was an understood thing that discipline was to be relaxed whenever their elder brother's holiday-time came round. However, seeing the abuse John made of his right to be idle, Ellen disdained to avail herself of hers and kept to her lessons more diligently than usual. Harry, who was four years John's junior, and therefore his persevering imitator, unless work of any kind was in question, always bore John company through the day ; hunting out a word for him occasionally in the dictionary, and joining very heartily in all his riotous demonstrations.

"I shall be so glad when you're back at school," John," sighed Ellen one morning, as she collected her books together.

"I'm much obliged to you, but I shan't; I like home best."

John was stretched on the ground at full length, working and amusing himself by turns as usual.

"I dare say you do," said Ellen; "you can't go on just as you please at school."

"And I should like to know whether I can here?" returned John with a grimace. "Come, have you let me have one peaceable half-hour all this week?"

Ellen disdained to answer, and turned to the bookshelves with her load.

"Besides, what more could I do if I were at school?" continued John. "What do you call this?" and he held up a book.

"Well, it ought to be work, but it isn't. I can't see what good it's going to do you."

"Can't you? But if I can get the contents of a book into my head without looking solemn over it, why shouldn't I?"

"I don't know. The thing is whether you can."

"And that's a question you won't be able to answer till you're well enough up in your Latin to put me through an examination. Just wait and see what papa says to the theme I've done this morning. Let's see, where did I put it? Why, Lenny, you tiresome monkey, if you're not tearing it up!"

"How should he know it from waste paper, if he

sees it on the floor?" said Ellen. "You ought to keep your things in their proper places."

But John's good humour was not to be disturbed. He made a great show of an intention to do battle with Lenny, at sight of which the little fellow entrenched himself behind a chair, and a desperate romp ensued.

"I suppose you've finished, then," said Ellen, "and I can put your things away?"

"No, I haven't," and John went panting back to his place. "Thanks to this little plague, I've all my work to do over again."

"Well, that won't take you long," said Ellen.

John caught up a stray sheet of paper, and worked away at the fresh theme with great diligence, till Harry, who was boat-building at the other end of the room, suddenly held up a small specimen of his workmanship for inspection.

"The mast isn't straight," said John, "and it will capsize as soon as you put it in water. Just fetch in a bucketfull and you'll see."

"It mustn't come in here, Harry," said Ellen, "you know papa wouldn't like it."

"Well, let's go out to the pond," said Harry.

The pond was a little piece of ornamental water in front of the house, the work of some former tenant, who had no little children to dabble their clothes at it, and run the risk of tumbling in half a dozen times a day.

"Well, I'm ready," said John, getting lazily upon his feet. "Now then, Lenny, what fresh mischief are you after? Come, I can't have my gum wasted."

" But I'm sticking your paper," lisped Lenny.

" So you are ; why, what a clever little man, to be sure. Only it's a pity that some of the bits are topsy turvy, and wrong side outwards, and I don't know how. Well, never mind, you and I have done enough for one morning, so we'll be off." And John perched Lenny on his shoulder, and strode off, followed by Harry.

The next minute a shout from Lenny raised to a pitch of ecstasy that portended mischief drew Ellen's attention to the window. There was the little fellow, sitting on the edge of the " pond," splashing the water over his clean frock and pinafore. She darted out to the rescue ; but, by the time the door was reached, John had already caught Lenny up, and was holding him out at arm's length, threatening to shake him till he was dry—a mode of punishment that the offender seemed to think he should greatly enjoy.

" O John ! it's too bad," said Ellen, " I think you do it all on purpose to vex me. Lenny, come in and have your things changed directly."

" No, I won't," said Lenny.

" But you must. John, put him down ! "

" O dear ! " said John, perching Lenny on his shoulder, to the great damage of his jacket ; " what a thing it is to be under such a tyrant."

" What's a tyrant ? " asked Lenny.

" A little girl in a prim apron, who makes a fuss about nothing."

" Oh ! that's Nelly."

This remark gave John and Harry so much amuse- ment that Lenny fancied he had said something extremely clever, and repeated it with the additional information that "he didn't care for what she said, and wasn't going to mind her."

"Put him down," said Ellen, stamping with passion. " It's shameful of you, John, to teach him to be naughty, and call me names."

" What is this ? " said Mr. Foster, advancing from the churchyard. "John, what are you doing with the child? "

"Teaching him to get into mischief, papa, and not mind what I say," was Ellen's explanation.

" That is very wrong, John," said Mr. Foster. " You ought to help your sister to keep him in order. Lenny, come here."

The child obeyed, and Mr. Foster took him into the house, and summoned Mary.

" You must put him to bed," he said, as the servant appeared, "and keep him there till his clothes can be dried."

" Hadn't I better get him out some others ? " said Ellen.

"No ; I wish him to understand that whenever he wets his clothes at the pond he must stay in bed until they are dried."

Lenny was led off sobbing up-stairs, and Ellen, who found it a difficult matter to keep back her own tears, followed her papa into the dining-room.

" Put on your hat, Nelly," said Mr. Foster, "and come for a walk with me."

" But will there be time, papa ? "

" Yes ; Mary can let us have our dinner a little later to-day."

Ellen gladly obeyed, and a few minutes after she was crossing the churchyard with her father.

"Oh! how nice it is to be alone with you again, papa," she said; "it seems so long since we have had a quiet half-hour all to ourselves."

"Yes; but as John is away from home for nearly ten months in the year, we mustn't grudge him our company during the other two."

"Well, I shouldn't mind if he would only behave himself; but he keeps us in a constant worry all day."

"Are you quite sure that there is no fault on your own side, Nelly?"

"O no, papa; there may be some, of course, for I can't help getting out of patience with him. But then he is so tiresome, and never minds what I say."

"Is it quite to be expected that he should? John is sixteen, I think, and you—"

"I am thirteen, papa; but as I have to be house-keeper, and see to everything— "

"But John is not one of the things that require seeing to, Nelly; he is quite capable of taking care of himself. I am afraid these housekeeping duties have quite turned your head. You had better give me back that great bunch of keys, and let me put it into my pocket again."

"O no; pray let me keep them, papa. I couldn't bear to give them up now."

"But if their possession quite spoils your temper, Nelly, what shall I do?"

"Oh! you always think that I am in fault, papa, and the boys right."

"No, I don't, indeed. John is very far from being a model of excellence, but the chief faults he has shown lately—love of fun and carelessness—are not very heinous ones in a boy of his age. Come, I want to turn down here."

They had reached a narrow lane leading to the village, and Ellen, who had expected to keep straight on to the fields, looked up with a very disappointed face.

"O papa, I didn't know you were going to the village. I thought you had been there all the morning."

"So I have, Nelly; but there's another visit still I want to pay."

Half way through the straggling street, Mr. Foster stopped before a cottage door, and said, as he lifted the latch—

"I don't think you've seen Hannah Norris lately, Nelly."

"No, papa, not since she has been ill."

They passed into a long red-bricked kitchen, looking very bright and airy with its clean casement window at each end. Round the further one, which looked out on the back garden, there was a group of children just home from morning school. They drew shyly aside as Mr. Foster entered, and Ellen saw a little girl about her own age lying on a bed. She looked very white and thin, but had a sweet cheerful face.

"I hope you are feeling better to-day, Hannah,"

said Mr. Foster. " Here is an old friend come to see you."

Ellen had often met Hannah before in the village, and at the Sunday school, so she held out her hand, and said she was sorry to see her so ill.

" Thank you, but I am better now—at least I don't suffer so much."

" And how can you bear all these noisy folks about you ? " said Mr. Foster ; "I could hear them before I got to the door."

" Oh ! I'm so glad to get them back, sir, that I don't mind their noise. The morning seems long, sometimes, when they're away."

" Well, I dare say it does if you are left quite alone. What do you do to amuse yourself ?"

" Oh ! a great many things, sir. Mother always leaves me work, and I take it up when I can ; and sometimes I read—"

" And she makes me daisy chains," said a little fellow, who was seized with a sudden panic as soon as the words were out of his mouth, and hid himself behind an elder sister.

" Well, that's very kind of her, Tom," said Mr. Foster ; " I see she has just finished one now. Come here and show it to me."

After a little pushing and whispering from the sister who formed Tom's screen, he took courage to come forward slowly, dragging his daisy chain. Once at Mr. Foster's side, he seemed to feel himself quite safe, and looked on in great delight while the chain was undergoing inspection.

K

"And she made me this," he said, holding out his pinafore.

"But you were only to show the daisy chain," said Hannah, colouring.

"And these socks," continued Tom, without heeding the interruption, "and some bigger ones for old Mary Field.   Polly and me took 'em round to her yesterday. She was so pleased to see 'em!"

"I dare say she was," and Mr. Foster drew little Tom upon his knee.   "But what made Hannah think of knitting stockings for old Mary?"

Tom looked towards his sister for an explanation, and Hannah answered, a little reluctantly, that her mother had said in the winter that poor old Mary sadly wanted warm stockings, as her feet were so cold; but she had not been able to get them done before.

"Because they was wool," put in Tom.

"Why, do woollen stockings take longer to knit than cotton ones?"

"Yes, when you've got it to get."

This reply requiring to be made a little clearer, Tom's eyes began appealing to Hannah.

"We bought it with our own pence," said Hannah, "and, as wool is very dear, one skein was often used up long before we could get another.—O Tom, we mustn't let you know what we're doing again."

But Tom had no idea of keeping secrets, and so he went on to inform Mr. Foster that Hannah meant to make another pair of stockings, so that old Mary might have a change.

" And are they to be woollen ones, too ? "

" Yes, just like the others."

" Then I think you must look out for a few more pence-holders to assist in buying the wool, or the old stockings will be quite worn out before the new ones can be finished. Suppose my little girl tries to spare you some of her pence now and then ? "

" Shall she ? " and Tom looked with a beaming face towards Hannah.

" If Miss Ellen pleases."

" Oh, I should like to very much," said Ellen, " and John shall give something, and Harry too. We'll get you lots of wool."

" But I can't knit very fast, Miss Ellen."

" But Polly can help you, and Jem and I will wind the skeins," said Tom, not thinking it wise to limit the promised supply.

" Do not be afraid, Hannah," said Mr. Foster, " the wool is not likely to come in faster than you can use it. Ellen shall bring it herself, and see how the stockings are getting on."

As soon as they were outside the cottage door, Ellen expressed her sorrow at the change that had taken place in Hannah since she saw her last, and asked her papa if he thought she would ever get any better.

" Yes, she has been mending for some time, Nelly ; but there's no hope, I fear, of her ever getting quite well again."

" I wonder how she manages to get through so much work. It never seems easy to do anything but read when you are lying down."

" No, but Hannah contrives to make herself very useful in a great many ways. Her mother told me, the other day, that she did more to help others than half a dozen healthy little girls. You must go and see her sometimes, Ellen."

" Yes, papa, I'll take her the wool as soon as I can get it."

Some time in the afternoon, Ellen told John that Hannah Norris was going to make some stockings for old Mary Field, and that she had promised they should all help to buy the wool.

" You shouldn't give away other people's money," replied John, without looking up from his book.

" But papa heard what I said, and he made no objection."

" Well, give your threepence."

" But that won't buy enough. You must help too, John. You oughtn't to be so selfish as to want to keep all your money to yourself."

" Thank you for the admonition, though it might have been put a little more politely."

" Then you don't mean to give any of your money ? "

" No, I've a way for every penny of it."

Ellen did not condescend to ask what the " way " was ; and so, as John went on comfortably with his reading, she thought him the most selfish, disagreeable boy she had ever seen.

When Saturday, the children's pay-day, came round, Ellen said, as she took her threepence of Mr. Foster,

" That is all there will be towards the wool this week, papa."

"What, your threepence, Nelly?"

"Yes; neither John nor Harry will give anything."

"But you must not part with all your money; half will, perhaps, buy quite as much wool as Hannah can knit up in the course of the week."

"Oh, I don't mind, papa." But Ellen's voice seemed to say that she did mind very much indeed.

"I am afraid you are not speaking the truth," said Mr. Foster, gravely. "If you cannot be a cheerful giver, it will be best to keep all your money to yourself. I always wish you to do as you like with it."

"O papa, I don't care for the money, I don't indeed! Only I am vexed to see John and Harry so selfish."

"Is that all? And how do you know they are selfish?"

"Why, papa, they must be if they can't afford to spend a penny of their money on any one but themselves."

"Certainly, but I do not see that we have proved that yet. It is clear they cannot spare any for Hannah's wool, but it does not necessarily follow that they are going to spend it all upon themselves."

The thought that her papa was always ready to take their part occurred again to Ellen, and though she did not say anything about it, Mr. Foster saw instantly what was passing through her mind.

"I do not think I have said more than they deserve, Ellen. With all his faults John is not a selfish lad. Perhaps he is saving up his weekly sixpences for books; he knows I cannot afford to buy him many."

"O no, papa, I heard him tell Harry that Mr. Carrysford said he was to use Edgar's books, and as they are in the same class he will not have to buy any."

"Ah, that was very kind ; John will get on famously!" And Mr. Foster relapsed into a pleasant reverie, in which old Mary Field's stockings seemed quite forgotten.

"Shall I put this away then for the wool, papa?" asked Ellen, holding up her threepence.

"No, I think you had better buy what you can with it at once, as Hannah may want to begin the stockings."

"But I had promised to take her so much."

"Yes, provided John and Harry contributed. But Hannah is a sensible little girl, and knows you cannot answer for any one but yourself. As you have done your part she will be quite satisfied."

Ellen followed her papa's advice, and found he was right. The threepenny skein of wool was larger than she had expected, and was received at the Norrises as a very munificent donation. Hannah declared that there was quite as much as she could knit up within the next week, and even Tom, whose expectations were on a more extensive scale, made no complaint.

When the next Saturday came round, Mr. Foster asked Ellen, as he handed her her allowance, if John intended to contribute anything that week towards the stockings.

"I don't know, papa."

"But haven't you asked him?"

"No, I thought one refusal was enough."

"But that was very foolish, Ellen. Do you remember

who it is that has said, 'I am meek, and lowly of heart?'"

"Yes, papa," replied Ellen, with downcast eyes.

"Then I think pride must be sadly unbecoming in us. Try to put it aside at once, Nelly, and ask John if he means to spare you any of his money this week."

It happened that John offered himself as Ellen's escort to the church that afternoon, and as she sat down for her hour's practice he stretched himself along one of the benches to enjoy a little lazy reading. The quiet church and sweet old psalm tunes soothed Ellen's ruffled temper, and by the time the practice was finished she was able to say in a tolerably gentle tone,

"Do you mean to spare anything for the wool this week, John?"

"No, I told you I couldn't."

"You said so last week, but I didn't know you always meant to keep your whole allowance to yourself."

"But I do—at least till I get what I want. What a fuss you make about that old woman's stockings, Nell! Why can't she wait?"

"She has only one pair to go on with, I believe; and then it will take Hannah a good while to make the other."

"And woollen stockings in the middle of summer, too! Who ever heard of such a thing? Tell her they're bad for her."

"But she's very old, John, and can't get about."

"Well, come to me when I'm back at Christmas, and I'll see what I can do."

"But then the summer would be round again before the stockings were finished."

"Oh, I forgot they had to be made. What a nuisance! Well, it can't be helped, Nell, for I am in debt now."

"But you ought not to be, John; papa would be very angry if he knew it."

"Oh, I dare say! Come, if you've finished practising we'll cut the lecture short and be off."

Ellen closed her instrument, and John, rolling off his uneasy couch, put his own and Ellen's book under his arm, and sauntered out of the church. In the porch they found Harry, looking flushed and mysterious.

"It's come!" Ellen heard him whisper to John, and the two boys ran off across the churchyard to the vicarage.

When Ellen went into the dining-room, her two brothers were sitting down to their work—a show of industry very unusual on a Saturday afternoon—and she glanced suspiciously round. What was it that had come, and was making John and Harry look so excessively wise and satisfied?—A toy? No, there was Harry's untidy play-box standing in one corner just as they had left it. A book? and her eyes wandered to the shelves. No, but something lying on the top—an unwieldy concern, with one sharp end projecting from its brown paper cover.

"So you have bought a ship with your money, John," she said.

"How have you found that out?"

"Why, I can see it; there's the mast sticking out."

" Dear me, how clear-sighted you are ! "   And both the boys laughed.

By the aid of a chair, her papa's writing-table, and a corner of the mantel-piece, forming a succession of steps, Ellen was in the habit of reaching books down from the top shelf, and she instantly mounted the ascent to get a nearer view of the mysterious package ; but, as she stretched out her hand to seize it, John's rising caused her, in her eager haste, to overbalance herself, and she slipped down, striking her back as she fell against the sharp edge of the writing-table.

" There ! " said John, going composedly back to his seat, " you'd better not try that again ! "

But Ellen continuing to lie quite motionless, just as she had fallen, he jumped up the next minute and tried to raise her, but a sharp cry of pain followed the attempt.

" My poor old Nell," said John, " I'm afraid you're hurt."

He put his arms round her again, this time more tenderly, and carried her to the sofa.   As he laid her down, he saw she had fainted.   Harry ran out for some water, and both boys were bathing her face when Mr. Foster came in.   Just then Ellen opened her eyes, and seeing only frightened looks about her, held out her hand to her papa, and tried to smile.

" It was my fault, papa ; I was climbing up to see John's ship."

" What ship ? "

" A new one that had been just sent in, and John had put it out of my reach."

"It wasn't a ship, papa," said John, huskily, "it was a book-rest that I had been saving up to get you."

"O John!" said Ellen, "and I've spoilt all the pleasant surprise you meant to give papa."

"Never mind, I shan't care for that, Nell, if you're not much hurt."

"No, I feel better now; it's only my back!"

"Only!" and Mr. Foster bent over her with anxious eyes.

He had not once thought of the book-rest, and Ellen was afraid John would feel disappointed.

"Get it down, John," she said, "and fix it on papa's chair."

John went through the ceremony with very little spirit, and then came back to Ellen's side.

"How do you like it, papa?" asked Ellen.

"Like what, my darling?"

"The book-rest. Oh, do look at it, papa!"

Ellen raised herself a little, in her eagerness to have John's present appreciated, but sank back again instantly with a pitiful cry of pain.

"Go for Mr. Deans, John," said Mr. Foster.

John hurried away; and Mr. Foster sat down at Ellen's side, took her hand in his, and told her she must be quite still for a while. Presently the doctor came, and, after a short stay, he left the room with Mr. Foster.

"What does he say?" asked Ellen, as her papa again took his place at her side.

"He can hardly ascertain the extent of the injury

yet, but he hopes it is only a slight sprain, and that you will soon be well again."

"I am so glad, papa! Oh, if I had minded what you said, this wouldn't have happened!"

"What do you mean, Nelly?"

"If I had tried to be patient, and not think that John was making a selfish use of his money, I shouldn't have climbed up to pry into his secrets. Papa! you haven't thanked him for the book-rest yet."

"No, but I will, Nelly. It was very kind of him to think of it."

At that moment John came in to hear what the doctor had said of Ellen, and after he had been told, Mr. Foster bethought himself of his present, and thanked John for it warmly. Then the chair was wheeled round, that Ellen might see how it looked with its new adornment, and Mr. Foster sat down in it, and made a great pretence of reading.

"You'll have no more weary chest-aches now, papa," said Ellen.

"No, I am afraid my reading will be made so easy to me now that I shall go to sleep over it."

But the next minute Ellen could scarcely keep back her tears, as she saw the book-rest thrust out of sight and forgotten again.

After a few days' attendance on Ellen, Mr. Deans began to think more seriously of her injury, and proposed that further advice should be sent for from London. Ellen was greatly distressed when she heard of this plan, and begged her father to wait a little longer before going to any further expense.

"But I want to get you well, my darling."

"And I really am better, papa. I walked quite round my room last night after John had taken me up."

"Yes, and nearly fainted afterwards, he told me. You mustn't do that again, Nelly.

"Very well, I won't, papa. I'll keep quite quiet, and do all Mr. Deans tells me. Only promise me not to send for any one else."

But Mr. Foster could not do that, and the next day the London physician came.

John was reading aloud to Ellen that evening, when his two schoolfellows, the Carrysfords, hurried in to say "good-bye," as they were going back to school the next day. Mr. Foster was out, and as the boys were unable to wait long they took leave of Ellen, saying they could look out for him as they passed through the village.

"But it won't matter if we miss him," said the elder Carrysford, "as he's sure to be at home when we call in for you, John, in the morning."

"Here, just stop a minute," said John, "and I'll go a bit of the way home with you."

He dashed about the room for his cap, which was never in its right place, and having found it at last, the three lads went out together.

Half-an-hour later John came panting back, and settled himself down to his book again.

"Oh don't read now, John," said Ellen. "I never thought of its being your last evening at home. Why didn't you tell me ? "

"Well, I didn't know that it was."

"What do you mean? All your things want looking to, you know. Oh, how could I be so thoughtless!"

"Well, never mind, there's no hurry. I'm not likely to be off just yet."

"Why not? what are you going to stay behind for?"

"Oh, nothing particular; only as I worked very hard last half I can afford to take a longer holiday now—that's all!"

"No, it's not, John; there's some other reason, I'm sure. What is it? you ought to tell me."

"But what does it matter? I shall have a fine time of it here! I can work and idle by turns, or do both together if I like, without having a creature to find fault with me."

"O John, I can guess what it is—the expense! I am costing papa so much now that he cannot afford to send you back to school. That's the real reason of your stopping at home, isn't it?"

"And won't you be glad to have me?" was John's evasive answer. "Who would you get to read to you after I was gone?"

"I don't want to be read to. O John, it's dreadful! I don't know how you can bear the sight of me!"

John laughed, and told her she was not very unpleasant looking, if she didn't cry and make a fright of herself—a hint to leave off sobbing that she was far too much distressed to notice.

When Mr. Foster came in, Ellen took the first opportunity of speaking to him about her fresh trouble, and asked him if it was necessary that John should stay at home that half.

"Yes, I am afraid so; your wants must come first now, Nelly."

"But it will be such a disappointment to John, papa, he thinks so much of his school."

"Yes, he will feel it, I know. But he is quite pre-pared to make the best of it, and to work as well as he can at home."

"Yes, he is very good. I don't know how I could ever think him selfish."

"Only by letting temper blind you sometimes. When we are not at peace with ourselves, Nelly, we are apt to judge unkindly of others."

"Yes, I see it all now. Do you remember talking to me about this, papa?" and Ellen drew from her pocket the little piece of silver ore that Mr. Foster had given her a few weeks before.

"Yes, I am glad to see that you keep it by you."

"But I didn't at first—at least not where I could see it, for I never liked to look at it when I was angry. O papa, if I had let my little trials teach me patience, I shouldn't have had this great one!"

"You would not have slipped and hurt yourself in anger, Nelly, but suffering might have come to you in many other ways. I do not wish you to take up the notion that it is sent to us simply as a punish-ment."

"O no, papa, I couldn't bear to think that! It would make it seem so much worse."

"God dealeth with us as with children. When I

correct you, Nelly, I hope you do not think that the only end I have in view is to punish you."

"O no, papa, it is to make me better! and I will try to learn now, I will indeed. Only it seems so hard that John should have to suffer too."

"Never mind ; if he doesn't complain you mustn't, Nelly, and Christmas will soon be here."

"But we don't know that he will be able to go even then, papa."

"We can't be sure of it, certainly. But I think present troubles are all we need concern ourselves about, and it is not well to make much even of them. Come, I must not let you get moped."

Mr. Foster lit the lamp, and the boys, seeing the light from the garden, came in and brightened the room with their fun and chatter. John took the chess-board to Ellen's side, and played with her till the supper-tray was brought in. Then, as they separated for the night, he took her up in his strong arms, and told her, as he mounted the stairs, that it was a good thing he was going to be at home, for she couldn't possibly do without him."

"And I used to say that I should be so glad to get rid of you, John."

"Yes, and you'll have good reason to tell me so half-a-dozen times more before my holiday is over."

"Well, I could say so now for some things, John, for I can't bear your having to stay at home. What did the Carrysfords say about it ? "

"Well, nothing, because I hadn't the courage to tell them, although I went out on purpose."

"Oh, what a pity! They'll be round for you in the morning."

"No, Harry took a note up to-night, so they know all about it now."

"And you haven't bid them good-bye!"

"No, but I shall. I mean to be down at the station before them in the morning. and see them off. There, now, you're all right, poor old Nell! I'll send Mary up to look after you. Good-night!"

Very early the next morning Ellen was left quite alone. Mr. Foster went out into the village, and the two boys had hurried off to the station, before she was up, to see their old friends start for school. She called Lenny to her to have his morning lesson, but before she had got far beyond the great A (which Lenny, staring hard at a grave-looking ass in the centre, would persist in saying stood for donkey), Mr. Carrysford bustled into the room.

"Oh, didn't you get John's note?" said Ellen, as he stooped down to shake hands with her.

"Yes, that's what I've come about. I never heard such nonsense in my life! Is your father at home?"

"No, sir; he's out somewhere in the village."

"And the boys—where's this precious John?"

"Oh, he's gone down to the station to see Tom and Edgar off."

"Then he'll have his journey for nothing, as they're both at home mending their fishing tackle. Will your father be long?"

"No. sir; he told me he should soon be back."

"Very well, then I'll wait for him," and Mr. Carrys-

Page 161.

ford sat down, and looked out of the window, till
Lenny suddenly shouting out the information that " B
stood for bun," made him turn round, and ask Ellen
what she was doing.

" Teaching Lenny his letters, sir."

" Dear me; what's the use of bothering yourself
now ? Sick people have no business to work."

" But I must do something to amuse myself."

" Oh, of course ; but can't you find anything better
than teaching ? Haven't you a doll to look after?"

" No, sir," answered Ellen, with a little flush of
wounded dignity, " I gave up dolls long ago."

" Did you ? oh, I suppose so. Well, what comes
next—crochet, isn't it ?"

" I don't know, sir," replied Ellen, thinking that
even a more objectionable occupation than doll-dress-
ing, " I never learnt such useless work."

Mr. Carrysford looked at Ellen as if he thought her
a very odd little girl. Then he took Lenny on his knee,
and tried to confuse his recently acquired knowledge
by turning the A upside down, and asking what it stood
for in that position.

" Donkey," replied Lenny, with great promptness.

" O Lenny, you know that's not right," said Ellen.

" But I don't see how he should," said Mr. Carrysford, " when there's the identical animal staring him
right in the face."

" But he knows that's not the name he ought to
give it."

" And what does V stand for ?" and Mr. Carrysford
turned a fresh page.

L

"Fiddle," replied Lenny.

"Famous! my man. How well you're getting on!"

"Oh, please don't," said Ellen, "you can't think what a trouble it is to teach him his letters."

"Then why don't you get a better book? How is a child to be expected to call a donkey an ass, or a fiddle a violin? Why I could make a more sensible A B C book myself. There, jump down, my man, I can see your father coming."

Lenny obeyed, and Mr. Carrysford went out to meet the vicar. The next minute Ellen saw them pass the window talking very earnestly together. They took a few more turns up and down the narrow path, and then went into the little parlour on the other side of the passage. Presently Mr. Carrysford came out again, shouted good-bye to Ellen as he passed her open door; and then Mr. Foster looked in to ask if John had returned.

"No, papa; I dare say he has waited for the next train, thinking the boys would start by that. But did Mr. Carrysford tell you they're not gone?"

"Yes, it seems they wouldn't leave John behind. What would you say, Nelly, to their going back together, after all?"

"Oh, I should be so glad, papa! But can you manage to let him?"

"Well, I shall have nothing to do with it. Mr. Carrysford very kindly tells me he intends to bear all John's school expenses till you are quite well again."

"But will John like that, papa?"

"Yes ; there is no humiliation in accepting a favour from such a kind old friend."

When John came in and heard of the arrangement he nearly went wild with delight. Every light article within reach that did not happen to be breakable was tossed up to the ceiling—a frantic demonstration, ending, to Lenny's supreme satisfaction, in the lodgment of his A B C book on some piece of furniture of unattainable height. It was some time before Ellen could get John to her side, to listen, as she said, to reason.

"Now, then, what is it?" he said, at last.

"Why, there are all your things to be got ready."

"Well, that won't take long ; I can stow them away in about five minutes."

"But they must be looked over and mended first. Would you mind fetching them down ? and then I'll see what I can do with them."

"Oh, nonsense, don't you bother yourself! If I come upon any terrible tatters when I'm packing, I'll get Mary to stitch them up."

"And she'll only make them worse ; she works so badly. Oh, do get them down, John ; there isn't a minute to lose."

John went very reluctantly, and presently returned, bringing a load of miscellaneous articles under each arm.

"There they are," and he threw them down at Ellen's side. "And now you'll want me to stay and thread your needles."

"No, I shan't ; that will be the easiest part of the business. O John ! how could you crumple up all this nice linen so ?"

L 2

"Dear me! I thought I was very careful. Well, what do you want—tape, scissors, cotton?"

"O no; pray don't touch that!" for John's unscrupulous fingers were plunging into the depths of Ellen's neat work-basket. "Lenny can get me all I want."

"Very well. Then I'll be off to the Carrysfords to see when we're to start."

As soon as John was gone, Ellen began her work of examination, taking the stockings first. They were in far worse condition than she had expected. Thin places abounded everywhere, and in some of them even holes. One unlucky pair presented such a forlorn appearance that, without looking any further, she took up her needle and cotton and set to work. Very slowly the first hole was filled up, and then she was obliged to put the stockings down again and rest both eyes and arms. Working in an entirely recumbent position is not easy, and Ellen did not like to sit up, as the doctors had forbidden her attempting to do so for some time to come. After a few minutes' rest she tried again, but got on this time so much worse than at first, that, as she laid the stocking down a second time, she began to cry bitterly over her own helplessness. Presently there was a gentle noise outside the door. Some one's hands—Lenny's, she supposed—were busy with the handle, and making very patient but fruitless efforts to turn it round.

"Come and open!" shouted a voice through the keyhole.

"But I can't; you must go to Mary."

The small hands outside went to work again, and at last the door yielded, and little Tom Norris walked in. Nobody had happened to see him as he entered the house, and so he had made his way into the parlour.

" Oh, I'm so glad to see you ! " said Ellen. " Come here, and tell me how Hannah manages to do her work, for I can't get on at all."

Tom stationed himself in front of Ellen, and stared at her with a face of great intentness. He was evidently giving the question his whole attention.

" Can't you sit up ? " asked Tom at last.

" No—at least I mustn't."

" Then that's it," said Tom ; " Hannah can."

There was no hope, then, and poor John would have to be sent back to school with his stockings unmended ! —an alternative so dreadful that Ellen cried over it more bitterly than ever. Tom stood by, in evident unconsciousness that she might not like to have her grief so closely watched, till the tears were dried, and Ellen looked up to ask how Hannah was.

" She's better," answered Tom, " and sent me to say that we're much obliged for the wool, and don't want any more."

" Are you quite sure, Tom ? "

" Yes, Hannah says so ; and she'll have the stockings done next week."

" Will she ? Oh, how I wish I could work like that ! But I'm no use at all now : I've been trying for the last half-hour to darn this stocking, and it isn't done yet."

" But can't it wait till you're better ? "

"No; John wants it to take back with him to school, and he's going to-morrow or the next day; and there's all this pile to be mended, and other things besides. I don't know what I shall do."

"I'll ask Hannah."

"No, don't bother her about it—O Tom, pray don't!"

But Tom had already started, and Ellen could do nothing but lie still and wait for his return. He soon came, carrying a little basket, and looking very hot and breathless.

"Hannah says I'm to take 'em back, and she'll do 'em," he gasped out.

"Oh! but I don't like to give her the trouble, Tom, she has so much to do."

"But she's put it all away, and now she's waiting for these. Can't I have 'em?"

"Well, just one pair, if you like—the one I've begun. She will be quite shocked to see so many holes."

"But I was to fill my basket, Hannah said."

"Did she? How kind she is! Then take what you like, Tom, and tell her I'll do as much for her when I get well."

Tom gathered all the stockings into his basket, and walked off with his load without a word. In the passage he was nearly upset by John, who came in the next minute, and asked Ellen "what that grave little man with the basket had to sell?"

"Oh! nothing, John," answered Ellen, laughing; "he's the dearest little fellow! You can't think what a service he has done me."

" Has he ? Well, I shouldn't have expected it from one of his size. Where did you pick him up ? "

" Oh, never mind that ! Who do you think is going to do your mending ? "

" Well, Mary, I should suppose—or, stop : perhaps your small friend has carried it off to the fairies."

" No ; he has taken it to Hannah Norris."

" What, the little girl who knits stockings for old women ? Why, that's famous ! Tell her she shall have all my money for wool when I come back at Christmas."

John's speaking of coming back reminded Ellen of the errand that had just taken him to the Carrysfords, and she asked him if he had heard when he was to start.

" Yes—the first thing to-morrow morning. And now I'm going to turn out all my books."

" Would you mind waiting till after dinner, John, as it's just time for Mary to come in and lay the cloth."

" O yes, of course. How thoughtless of me to forget ! "

A week or two before, Ellen's remonstrance would have been made in no very gentle tone, and John would probably have answered that he should do as he pleased—so true is it that "grievous words stir up anger."

In the afternoon John got out his books, and he and Harry began the packing. Like everything else they undertook together, it was carried on in the midst of a great deal of fun and romping ; but, having no-thing to do but to lie still and look on, Ellen could laugh at their proceedings as heartily as they did themselves. Her mind was quite at rest about the packing. Hannah, she knew, would do her part, and all the rough work had been made over to Mary, who promised to do her best with it. The linen only required a few buttons, and the repairing here and there of a frayed cuff or collar—little matters that she thought she could get through herself in the course of that long afternoon ; but, while she was threading her first needle, John caught up the whole pile of work at one sweep of his arms, and dashed off with it up-stairs. She was half disposed to be angry ; but it was John's last day at home, so she submitted pretty quietly, and could hardly help laughing the next minute, as he seized on her box of buttons, and told her he meant to stitch them all on so tightly the first half-holiday he got, that they would never come off any more. John's next exploit was to fetch down his box—a business that was got through with so much pulling and banging, and fighting with Harry to keep out of the way, that by the time it was successfully brought to an end he had to lie down on the floor to refresh himself for renewed exertion. Then books were collected and tumbled into his box—to form, as he said, a good solid substratum ; but, when that was done, it was found that the question of ownership had been so little attended to, that they had to be routed out again, and a grand fight ensued before the stolen property could be rescued. Much to Lenny's dismay, the unlucky A B C book, which had been dislodged from its high resting-place a few minutes before, turned up again in the scramble, and John tossed it to the other end of the room, asking "who had dared to put a work of such an elementary description into his box ?"

"I didn't," answered Harry.

"Perhaps it dropped in," suggested Lenny.

"Yes, out of your fingers," said Ellen.   "O Lenny, that was very naughty!   I am afraid you wanted to lose your book."

"You incorrigible little dunce!" and John held Lenny aloft, and administered to him a solemn lecture on the propriety of his sticking to his letters.

"But Mr. Carrysford says they're bad ones," said Lenny.

"What does he mean ?" asked John.

Ellen explained, and John undertook, at once, to get out cardboard and colours, and manufacture a fresh set that evening.   Then, as he set Lenny on his feet again, he told him seriously to be a good boy while he was away, and not give poor Nelly any trouble.

The packing went on more steadily after that.   The books were stowed quietly away, and Lenny was kept trotting to and fro after the different articles entrusted to Mary's skill—the "rough work," which proved, on inspection, to be very rough indeed.   Before that was packed, Tom Norris appeared at the door, shyly bringing in his little basket.

"Oh, I didn't expect you back yet," said Ellen. "How quick Hannah has been."

"But Jane helped her, and I threaded the needles."

"Why, what an industrious party you are!" said John.   "Here, come and empty your load into this box, my man."

Tom obeyed, and then asked to have his basket refilled.

" What with ? pears ? " asked John.

" No, mending.   There's a lot of it somewhere."

" Oh, I've taken possession of that to keep me out of mischief in holiday time.   Now, sit down, and I'll give you a slice of cake."

" But I mustn't stop.   Hannah's waiting."

" Oh, never mind that !   She's done enough work for to-day, and a nice rest will do her good.   There, when you've eaten that, I'll put a few slices in your basket for you to take home."

Tom accepted the proffered piece of cake, and sitting down at Ellen's side, proceeded to dispose of it at his leisure.

" I am so glad Hannah is getting better," said Ellen. " Does the doctor think she will soon be well ? "

" I don't know ; but her knee is beginning to heal."

" Oh, that's a good thing.   Can she stand on it yet ? "

" No, but she could if she'd got crutches."

" And is she to have them ? "

" Yes," answered Tom, quietly, " as soon as we can get 'em."

" As soon as you can get them ? " said John.   " And pray how much are they to cost ? "

" Three and sixpence.   I and Jane went down to Harry Lee's about it, and that's what he said they'd be."

" But how are you to get all that together ? " asked Ellen.

"Like as we did the wool," replied Tom.

"Of course," said John : "a subscription's the thing. Why, what a sharp lad you are ! I declare, when I give my first public lecture, I'll send you round with the plate."

"What does he mean ? " asked Tom.

"That you are a kind little boy to help to get Hannah's crutches. You must have my threepence towards them this week, Tom, as you won't want it for the wool."

"When shall I fetch it ? " asked Tom.

"On Saturday morning," said John. "It's due at twelve o'clock, and you must be here to the minute."

Tom promised he would, and then, having finished his piece of cake, he asked if the other slices were ready, as he wanted to go. John dashed about in a great bustle, and gave him, in addition to the cake, such a flourishing message of thanks for Hannah, that Tom had to go again, in considerable mystification, to Ellen, to know what he meant.

That last evening of John's at home seemed a little sad, though the making of the comical alphabet gave him and Harry plenty to do, and caused occasionally a good deal of laughing, in which every one joined, except the young gentleman for whose edification it was specially intended.

The first thing Ellen saw the next morning, as John laid her carefully on the sofa, was the book-rest, nicely fitted by some ingenious contrivance on the back.

"O John," said Ellen, turning away her eyes, "I don't think I shall ever be able to use it."

"O yes, you will! I couldn't bear the thought of your having to lie here sometimes with nothing to amuse you while I was away. Look, it will hold the book just where you want it."

"Yes, it is very nicely managed. How hard you must have worked this morning"—for two neat leather pads filled up each side of the sloping edge of the sofa.

"Yes," said Harry, sleepily; "he began bothering about it before five o'clock."

Soon after breakfast, the Carrysfords' carriage drove through the gate, and John's box was dragged out in the midst of some vigorous shouting from Harry and Lenny. Then John ran back into the dining-room to give Ellen a parting kiss.

"Good-bye, dear old Nell. Christmas will soon be here." And the next minute he was gone.

The rest of the morning was very trying to Ellen. Mr. Foster had an engagement which took him from home for the whole day; and Harry and Lenny had gone through too much excitement that morning to be very pleasant companions when it was all over. She was very glad, early in the afternoon, to see Tom Norris's round, satisfied face peering in at the open door. "I've come to tell you we shan't want your threepence on Saturday," he said.

"Why, isn't Hannah going to have her crutches?"

"Yes, but we haven't got to pay for 'em. Harry Lee was round this morning to see how big she'd want 'em, and he said Mr. John had done it."

"What, paid for them—are you quite sure?"

"Yes, ain't you glad?" for Ellen was looking a

little distressed at the thought that John was running in debt again.

" O yes, I am very glad that Hannah is going to have her crutches."

" What is it that you don't like, then?"

" Well, never mind now, Tom. Come here and tell me if there's anything else you'd like to save up for."

" No, nothing," answered Tom, without moving an inch from his station in the doorway. " What shall I say to Hannah?"

" Give her my love, and tell her I hope she will come and see me·when she can walk as far as this."

" Yes, she'll come ;" and Tom trotted off.

The next minute there was a great uproar outside— loud shouts from Harry and Lenny, and screams of affright from little Tom. Ellen rang her hand-bell, and called out to know what was the matter, but her voice was lost in the clamour, and every instant Tom's screams grew shriller. At last she could not bear to hear them any longer, and getting off her sofa she ran out into the garden. There was Harry standing on the edge of the pond, and holding little Tom over it at arm's length.

" O Harry, Harry, how can you!" said Nelly.

Harry started round on hearing her voice, and loosening his hold of Tom, the little fellow was struggling the next moment in the water. Fright prompted Ellen to make an effort to save him, but as her hand grasped his pinafore she sank back fainting on the gravel path. Fortunately Mary ran round, just then from the back garden, and her strong arms went to work with great energy to repair the disasters. Tom was dragged out of the water, and Ellen was carried back to the sofa, where she lay for some time looking almost lifeless. Harry and Lenny skulked off as soon as they saw the mischief they had done; but Tom kept close to Ellen's side, asking her every time she opened her eyes if she felt well again.

"Yes," gasped Ellen, at last, "I'm better now. Do see to him, Mary, his clothes are soaking."

But Tom refused to be touched. Hannah would dry him, he said, and if those boys were gone he would rather run home to her. Mary went with him part of the way, and then came back to see to Ellen. Shortly after Mr. Foster returned, and, at the first glimpse of Ellen's white face, he asked what had happened.

"Oh, not much, papa; I've only been frightened. Little Tom Norris was here just now, and fell into the water."

"Fell in," repeated Mary, who was standing by; "Master Harry put him in, you mean." And she told Mr. Foster how the mishap had occurred.

"Where is Harry?" asked Mr. Foster.

"He went off with Lenny, sir, as soon as it was all over."

"O papa, you won't punish him?" said Ellen, as she saw Mr. Foster moving towards the door.

"I can't help it, Ellen. Cowardice and cruelty are terrible faults, and must be checked."

Mr. Foster was away a long time, and when he came back he looked very pale and sad.

" My poor motherless boys !" he said ; "it's a sad grief to me to be obliged to punish them."

" I am sure Harry did not mean to put Tom into the water, papa ; he was only in fun."

" I can't understand fun at the expense of others, Nelly ; there is no excuse for him. I must go down to the Norrises and see how little Tom is."

" But you are tired, papa ; won't you wait for tea ? "

" No, I should not like them to think that I could treat such gross misconduct lightly. Mary can bring the tea in now, and I shall soon be back."

Mr. Foster returned shortly after, looking a good deal relieved.

" The Norrises are kind people," he said. " They were making all sorts of excuses for Harry, and seemed very much concerned about you."

" And how was little Tom ?"

" As bright as a bird. He was wrapped up in shawls at Hannah's side, and in that snug position seemed rather to enjoy the idea of having had an adventure. Hannah was full of gratitude for John's thoughtful present."

" Oh, then it is all right, papa. I was afraid you did not know anything about it."

" How do you mean, Nelly ?"

" Why, I knew John had not any money to spend, and so I thought he must have been running in debt."

" No ; Mr. Carrysford insisted on filling John's pockets as he does his own boys' before they go back to school, so that he had money enough to pay what was owing on the book-rest, and get Hannah's crutches besides. I believe he ordered a better pair than little Tom had been bargaining for."

" How good he is ! I have missed him so much to-day ; if he had been at home Harry would not have got into all this trouble."

" No ; John generally contrived to keep him out of mischief. I must see what I can do now, Ellen, for I cannot have you running such risks again."

Ellen tried to make light of the pain she was suffer-ing, but Mr. Foster could see that it was sometimes very acute, and he was not sorry when Mr. Deans, who had heard of Tom's adventure in the village, came in later in the evening to ascertain how his patient was going on.

Harry chose to come out the next day from his place of banishment with the idea that Ellen had injured him. If she had not pounced out upon him, he thought to himself, in wrathful despondency, he should not have dropped Tom into the pond, and then if she had not been so ridiculous as to go after him, and get ill, he, Harry, would not have been lectured and punished. Brooding over these wrongs, and being further exas-perated by the fact that his companions and pleasant holiday time were gone together, and that nothing but lessons and solitude loomed in the future, he became so disagreeable that Ellen found it a hard matter some-times to bear with him. Being naturally thoughtful, and rendered still more so by having little else to do than lie quiet and observe what passed around her, she was more troubled by the fear that Harry was going wrong than by all the discomfort he caused her in other ways. Mr. Foster was more than usually occupied, just, then, with parish matters, and, as Harry contrived to keep up a tolerably fair appearance before him, he was far from suspecting how he gave way to sloth and ill-temper during the greater part of the day.

"O Harry!" Ellen gently expostulated one morning, when she found that, not satisfied with neglecting his own lessons, he was bent on disturbing the alphabetical studies of Master Lenny, "you know you ought to be at your work."

"Well, so I am ; here are all my books spread out before me."

"But you are not attending to them ; you have been idling all the morning."

"And working too. John used to do both at once, why shouldn't I ?"

"Oh ! but he did a great many things that you and I couldn't. Papa would be very angry if he knew how you spent your time while he is away."

"Well, why don't you tell him, and get me into trouble ? I give you leave."

Ellen kept silent, certainly the wisest thing she could do just then, as Harry was evidently not disposed to listen to reason. Perhaps it would have been better had she told her papa, sometimes, how Harry went on during his absence ; but some feeling of honour deterred her from what she denominated telling tales, so she brooded over her troubles in silence—an occupation that did not, as in Harry's case, affect her temper, though it did her health very sadly. Lying on

that hard sofa, day after day, in helplessness and suffering was very trying, especially in her father's absence.
The Carrysfords took care that she should always have
a bunch of freshly-cut flowers at her side, and some
pleasant volume on the book-rest before her; but
Ellen's eyes often tired of both, and she would close
them, to wonder how long she was going to be such a
trouble to everybody, and to long earnestly for the kind
mother's watchful care that had kept everything in the
house so smooth and pleasant.

One afternoon she was roused by hearing somebody
coming up the path in an unusually laboured, noisy
way. She knew instantly who it was, and looked up
with a bright smile as Hannah Norris entered the
room. For a minute the two girls could hardly speak.
Then Hannah tried to say how sorry she had been
to hear of Ellen's accident, but stopped suddenly as
she saw her eyes filling with tears.

"We seem to have changed places, Hannah, don't
we?" said Ellen, trying to smile again. "But I am so
glad to see you. I have been looking for you every
day."

Hannah explained that she had not been able to
get so far before; and then she told Ellen in her
bright, quiet way, of her thankfulness at being about
again, and her gratitude for Master John's kindness.
Ellen would have liked to unburden her own mind in
return, but she was a little shy of Hannah at first, and
it was not until she had paid her several visits, and
found how good and true she was, that she ventured to
enter on the subject of her home anxieties.

"How is it that little Tom always minds all you say, Hannah?" was her introduction.

"Oh, I don't know; I suppose it's because he likes me."

"Well, but Lenny likes me, and yet he never cares for anything I say to him. O Hannah, you can't think what a trouble he and Harry are to me! They idle away their time dreadfully, and disobey all papa's orders as soon as he is out of sight."

"Yes, Master Harry hasn't gone on so well since Mr. John's been away. We've all noticed that."

"Why, what have you seen, Hannah?"

"Well, he gets with bad boys. There's Jem Long and Mat Lee he's very thick with, and they're the worst in the village."

"O dear, what would papa say if he knew it."

"But won't you tell him, Miss Ellen?"

"No, he has so much to vex him; and then I don't like Harry to say I tell tales and get him into trouble."

"I shouldn't mind that, Miss Ellen, if I was doing right; and Mr. Foster would rather be vexed a hundred times, I'm sure, than have Master Harry go wrong."

"Yes, I know that, and I must tell him if Harry doesn't get better."

"It's no use waiting for that, Miss Ellen, while he's about with Jem Long and his set. I'd speak out at once."

Ellen made no answer, and Hannah kept on for a minute or two with her work—a little frock she was

M 2

mending for Lenny. Then she looked up with brightening eyes.

"There's Mr. John you might tell, Miss Ellen. He wouldn't make a trouble of it for five minutes, and I dare say Master Harry would mind what he said."

"Well, he might, Hannah ; at all events, I can try."

That evening Ellen pencilled, with some difficulty, a long letter to John, and asked her papa, who was writing near, to direct it. A few days after, a bulky package addressed to Harry came in with the morning letters, and Mr. Foster passed it over to him as he sat down to breakfast. Harry opened it eagerly, but after glancing over the first page, Ellen saw him colour and put the letter into his pocket. Directly breakfast was over he went away, and did not come back until Mr. Foster had gone out. He looked very sullen, and went round, without speaking, to his favourite corner by the window, which was just behind Ellen's sofa. He was so quiet for the next half hour that, not being able to peep over at his retreat, she began to fancy he must have passed out of the window. However, Harry was still in his corner, gloomily meditating, and at last he startled Ellen, by saying gruffly—

"So you've been complaining of me again. I just wish you would leave me alone."

"But I can't, Harry, while you go on so badly. It wouldn't be kind of me, indeed."

"Wouldn't it? Well, I'd rather you kept such kindness to yourself. And who told you I was always running after the Longs and Mat Lee, I should like to know ? "

Ellen did not think it wise to tell him ; however, the next minute Harry answered the question for himself.

"It was that nasty Hannah Norris, who is always coming spying round here. But I'll soon let her know that it will be safer for her to keep away."

"Then you don't mean to take John's advice, and try to do better ? "

"Never you mind, it's no business of yours."

"But it is, Harry," answered Ellen, with difficulty keeping back her tears. "I can't bear to see you going on so from day to day ; and if you don't mind what John says, I must tell papa—I must, indeed."

Instead of any answer, a furious burst of sobs came from Harry's corner, but Ellen only listened to them with a pained, weary look, for a fit of crying from him was never a hopeful sign. It only meant that he was making a desperate pretence of being contrite and full of good intentions.

But the pretence was so well kept up for a few days, that Ellen began to think, at last, it must be something better, and told Hannah, on her next visit, that John's letter had done Harry a great deal of good. But Hannah only shook her head very doubtfully over the information, for she had seen him in the village, where he was less on his guard, and had no reason to believe in the genuineness of his reformation. At home, however, the improvement was so marked that, when the lesson books were being put away on the following Saturday, Mr. Foster commended him for having been more attentive to his studies that week, and Ellen was very glad she had not vexed her papa with any dismal tales of Harry's misdoings.

The next day Mr. Foster gave his monthly sermon to the young, and as he sat by Ellen in the pleasant summer twilight, she told him how sorry she had felt at not being able to hear it.

"Then you shall have it now, if you like."

"Oh, thank you papa, if you are not too tired. Harry, don't go away," for Harry was slipping round to the door.

"Well, but I've heard it."

"Never mind that, Harry," said Mr. Foster, "if I don't mind preaching a sermon twice, I think you need not grudge the trouble of listening."

Harry sat down again, and then Mr. Foster gave them very simply and pleasantly the chief points of his sermon, and the striking illustrations he had introduced here and there, to make them plain to his little hearers. Any one listening to him might have fancied he was reciting one of Todd's sermons to children—those bright loving addresses that many little people find far more entertaining than their pleasantest stories. After he had finished, there was a short silence, and then Ellen said—

"Papa, I have been thinking we ought to do all we can to help you in your work."

"How do you mean, Nelly?"

"By showing that your teaching has not been thrown away on us."

"Certainly; that would be the best way of bringing it home to others. My preaching will be to little purpose, unless we all do our best to act up to it."

"Let us try this week to be more careful about our duties, Harry," said Ellen. "I dare say we shall find a great many wrong things to correct when we once begin. Will you see what you can do ?"

"O yes, I'm ready."

Ellen had to remind him very often of his promise in the course of the week, but, having done pretty well, and been commended for it by his papa, he was quite satisfied with himself. So the studies were neglected again for out-door rambles, as soon as Mr. Foster was away from home; and, before long, the pleas for exemption from punishment for ill-prepared lessons— shuffling excuses at first—became positive untruths.

"I couldn't do it, papa," was the unblushing assurance with which he would take back a returned lesson, "I had to go to town on an errand for Mary;" when the fact often was, that after looking and waiting for him an hour or more, Mary had been obliged to put her work aside, and fetch whatever was wanted herself. Ellen often remonstrated with him afterwards for his falsehoods with tears of shame, but he only laughed at her, calling her regard for truth girl's nonsense.

"I shall have to tell papa you haven't kept your promise, Harry," said Ellen, as the Sunday for the children's sermon was close at hand again.

"Well, you can't tell him more than he knows, for he was scolding me last night for idleness."

"Oh, why don't you try to please him, Harry ? you know how many things he has to vex him."

" Well, I'll try to-day. You shall see how industrious I can be."

Harry took down his books, and retreated with them to his favourite corner behind the head of Ellen's sofa. Presently there came a low whistle somewhere from the garden, which was instantly answered by Harry.

" Who are you whistling to ?" asked Ellen.

" Why, a dog to be sure.—Here, Snap ! Snap !"

A great rough dog ran panting into the room, and, leaping on Ellen's sofa, glared at her with open mouth.

" O Harry, call him off !" shrieked Ellen.

But Harry only stood by laughing ; and the dog, making a furious dash at the book-rest, sent that and the little vase of hot-house flowers that stood near it crashing down. Then, as the next rush seemed likely to be at Ellen's frightened face, Harry thought fit to call him away ; but he still kept up her fears by allowing him to prowl about the room as he pleased.

" Isn't he a beauty ?" he asked, as Ellen was shrinking back again from the near approach of the dog's fangs.

" No, he's a horrid brute ! If you don't get him out of the room, Harry, I must ring for Mary."

" And I'll set him at her if you do ; he's the dog to give a good grip ! Ben Stiggins says there isn't his match anywhere."

" Ben Stiggins, that dreadful fighting man ! You surely don't know anything about him ?"

" Well, I can't help it when he's always about the village ; besides, he's not so bad as people say.—Here, Snap, you must be off, my boy."

This command was not given to ease Ellen's fears, but because the whistle outside, which had been repeated several times, was growing loud and impatient.

"Here, this way, old fellow," said Harry, edging round to the window."

"But you're not going, Harry, are you?" said Ellen.

There was no answer, and Ellen rang her bell for Mary, thinking it would be a great relief to have the window behind her closed against the cold November wind, and any further intrusion from the redoubtable Snap.

"Master Harry's getting a bad boy," said Mary, as she picked up the fragments of the broken vase, "there's no end to the mischief he does in the house now."

"But he didn't do this, Mary; some great dog threw it down."

"Then he shouldn't have let the dog in. And now he's gone out just as dinner's ready."

"Never mind, Mary, I can wait."

"No you can't, nor Lenny, either, and master said you was to have it punctual, so I shall bring it in."

Mary kept her word, and then stayed to carve—a duty that had fallen of late to Harry's share whenever Mr. Foster was away, and which Mary, not deeming it within her province, undertook very unwillingly. Perhaps Lenny had most reason to complain of the arrangement, for Mary's eyes were very sharp, especially when she was cross, in detecting his little improprieties of behaviour; and, during the progress of dinner that day, her admonitions were accompanied with such constant threats of "no pudding," that the meal altogether was made rather uncomfortable to him. Ellen did not quite approve of such a mode of discipline, thinking it calculated to produce greediness ; however, it certainly was most effective.

Soon after dinner was over, and Lenny's mind at rest, for the time, on the subject of pudding, there was an impatient thumping at the kitchen-door, and Tommy Norris ran in, looking very hot and breathless.

" I came off as soon as ever they'd gone !" he said ; " I told Hannah I would."

"As soon as who had gone, Tom? what do you mean ?"

" The boys, and the great dog that flew at Hannah. I watched them all across the church meadows, and then ran off to tell you."

" What boys were they, Tom ? "

" The Longs and Master Harry. They set the great dog upon Hannah just as she got near the gate, and that was why she did not come to-day," and little Tom panted with breathlessness and eagerness till his complexion was something quite alarming to look at.

" Sit down quietly, and tell me all about it," said Ellen ; " I hope Hannah isn't hurt."

" No, but the great dog tore her frock, and rolled all the handkerchiefs she'd been hemming for you in the mud. Now she'll have to wash 'em before she can bring 'em back."

" Oh, I am so sorry ; but are you sure the boys set the dog on her ?"

" Yes, Hannah said so. She saw Master Harry and

Jem Long do it. Now I'll go, because Hannah will be frightened."

" No, stay a minute, Tom, and Mary shall give you something, and see you safe down the lane."

" Yes, you shall have Harry's pudding," said Lenny, who thought the owner had justly forfeited all title to it.

" No, we must not give what does not belong to us, Lenny," said Ellen. " There's a piece of cake in the cupboard that was put away for your supper to-night. Suppose you fetch Tom that."

Lenny was not quite prepared for this sacrifice : however, his mind was relieved, the next minute, by hearing Tom say that he could not stay. The fear of being attacked by the " great dog " was strong enough to shut out every other consideration, even to the weighty one of relinquishing a nice slice of cake. So Lenny was despatched into the kitchen to see if Mary could go with him part of the way home, an errand on which he set off very nimbly, and the next minute Mary came into the room and took Tom under her protection, with a kindliness of manner that no one could have expected from her, who had seen the grim front with which she had awed Lenny into good behaviour during dinner-time.

Ellen spent an anxious afternoon looking eagerly for Harry, who, she hoped, would be able to say something in his own justification, and so give her an excuse for putting off the disagreeable duty of telling her papa of his misdoings. Mary came in now and then, to attend to the fire, but she made no comment on Hannah's adventure. She had already expressed herself, more than once, very emphatically, to the effect that "Master Harry was going to the bad," and took every fresh confirmation of that statement as something quite in the proper course of things. Very soon the November day came to an end, and then, after a miserable hour of almost total darkness, Mary brought in the tea things, and lit the lamp.

"You haven't seen anything of Harry yet, Mary ?"

"No, Miss Ellen."

"Is it tea-time already ? I did not know it was so late."

"Well, it's half-past five ; but it won't be tea-time to-night till master comes in."

Left to herself again, Ellen found it a hard matter to lie still and be patient. What would her papa say, when he came home and found Harry had been absent during the greater of the day ; and, worse still, when he discovered that he had, for some time past, been getting into bad company, and that she had kept the knowledge of it from him ? The sound of the first footfall on the gravel path was eagerly questioned in the hope that it might be Harry's ; but the step came on heavily, and the next minute Mr. Foster came into the room, very weary from a five miles' walk across rough country roads. Almost his first words were,—

"Where is Harry ?"

"He has not come in yet, papa."

There was nothing to alarm in that, as Harry was often out later on some of those domestic errands he was in the habit of bringing forward occasionally as an excuse for ill prepared lessons ; so Mr. Foster put on the warm slippers Mary had laid in the fender for him, and talked pleasantly to Ellen till he drew his chair up to the table, and so brought himself close to her side. Then he saw something was the matter, and connected it instantly with Harry's absence. "Has Harry been delayed?" he asked; "did you expect him back sooner?"

"Yes, papa ; at least, I did not know what to think. He went out just before dinner-time, and we have not seen him since."

"And you have no idea where he is gone?"

"No, papa. But—but I am afraid it is not all right."

"What do you mean, Ellen?"

"He was seen this morning crossing the church meadows with some bad boys—the Longs I think."

"But he cannot have made their acquaintance all at once. Have you suspected his getting into bad company before?"

"Yes, papa, Hannah Norris said something about it."

"And why haven't you told me?"

"I didn't like to vex you, papa."

"You have been very wrong, Ellen."

"Yes, I know I have," answered Ellen humbly, and worn out by her afternoon's worry, she could not suppress a few bitter sobs.

The comfortable slippers were exchanged for the wet boots again, and Mr. Foster went out. About an hour after he came back, looking so pale and unhappy, that Ellen saw he had heard no good report of Harry in the village. It was getting very late then, so tea was made, and, as he took his own cup, Mr. Foster sat listening to every sound outside; and more than once, when the wind swept the dead leaves along, he hurried out to the front door, fancying he heard Harry's stealthy tread on the path.

After another anxious hour, Mary suddenly appeared at the open door.

"I haven't heard any one come in," she said, "but there's a foot moving about over head."

Mr. Foster went up-stairs, and, for the next few minutes, loud outcries and lamentations issued from Harry's room. But he was not being hurt, for Mr. Foster had never been known, so far, to lift his hand in anger against one of his children.

He looked very sad when he came down again; and, after sitting for a few minutes in silence, he told Ellen to let him hear all she knew of Harry's doings since John had been gone. Ellen went through the dismal recital very unwillingly—from Harry's cowardly treatment of little Tom to his setting the dog on Hannah that morning. She would have been glad to spare her papa some of the miserable details, especially Harry's unblushing falsehoods; but, whenever she faltered, Mr. Foster's questions led her on, and obliged her to state the whole truth.

"If I had known something of this sooner, Ellen," said Mr. Foster, "a great deal of the mischief that has followed would have been prevented. You have been very wrong to hide Harry's faults from me."

"Yes, papa, but I hoped every day that he would mend. I did it for the best, indeed."

"But you made a great mistake. Suppose Harry

had had some deadly ailment, working its way deeper day by day, would you have thought it right to keep me in ignorance of it ? "

" O no, papa, of course not."

" Then surely a moral evil ought to have given you equal alarm. You see you have left Harry's faults to time and chance till they have taken such deep hold that it will be a hard matter now to subdue them. I must stay at home more, for a while," continued Mr. Foster, after a minute's silence. " It will be difficult to manage, with all my parish duties, but my children's welfare must come first."

" Couldn't you let Harry go to John's school, papa ? " said Ellen. " Mary is so careful, and I am getting well enough to do without a doctor now."

" No, home restraints will be safest for him till he can be trusted. A large school with its strong temptations to evil, and, to a certain extent, superficial disci pline, would be no place for him now."

" But John would take care of him, papa."

" He would do what he could, I know ; but boys in different classes cannot be much together. No, I see nothing to be done but to undertake him myself, Nelly, and do the best I can."

Very often during the next few weeks Mr. Foster thought he must give up, and send Harry at any risk to school. It was weary work struggling with him, for restraint only seemed to harden him, and he was always ready with some cunning shift to avoid it. The first time Mr. Foster took the precaution, before going out, of locking him up in his room, he was making his

way down by means of a large chestnut-tree near his
window before his papa could have reached the churchyard gate, and Mary burst into the dining-room to tell
Ellen what he was doing.

The window behind her sofa was just under the one
in Harry's room, and as Ellen raised herself up, and
looked out, she saw the lower branches of the chestnut
swaying to and fro under Harry's weight.

"Will you open the window, Mary," said Ellen, "I
must speak to him."

The sash was thrown up, and Ellen called out to beg
Harry to "go back to his room, and not to vex papa by
getting away when he was out." The boughs were quiet
for a minute; then Harry dropped down, and asked
her sulkily, "What she was making such a fuss for?"

With some difficulty Ellen persuaded him to come in,
and when she had him quietly beside her she tried to
make him understand how wrong it was not to bear
punishment patiently.

"But how would you like to be locked up?" said
Harry.

"Oh, not at all, of course, but papa won't lock you
up any more when he finds he can trust you. O
Harry, how can you grieve him so? What would
mamma say if she were here?"

This was touching Harry on a very tender point, for
he had dearly loved his mother. For a little while his
sobs were so quiet that Ellen thought they really did
mean something hopeful, and she ventured to ask him
if he would mind going back to his room, and letting
Mary lock him in again.

" No, if you won't tell papa."

" But I can't promise that, Harry, it wouldn't be right to deceive him. But when he hears you went back of your own accord he won't be angry, I'm sure."

Harry went, looking very repentant, and, the next minute, Mary put an astonished face in to announce that " Master Harry had let himself be locked up as meek as a lamb ! "

Ellen was very glad to have a more favourable report to make of him when Mr. Foster came in, and as soon as he had heard it he went up-stairs to release Harry from confinement. But he was already gone ! On being left to himself his good resolutions had fled ; and a passing glimpse of Snap, or a whistle from his master, had proved too strong a temptation to resist.

" But I think he meant to do right, papa," said Ellen, after she had heard of Harry's disappearance.

" I have no doubt he did, but you see other influences were at work as soon as he got away from you. Poor boy ! I don't know what I shall do with him."

They were expecting John and the two Carrysfords home in about a fortnight, and Ellen reminded Mr. Foster of their return, saying she thought that as soon as they were back Harry would give up his bad companions.

" For the time, no doubt ; but John will not be with us beyond ten days at the most, and then Harry will be thrown on his own resources for amusement again."

" Oh, if he could but go back with John, papa ! "

" But he can't, Nelly. I begin to see now that the plan would be advisable, but it isn't practicable. I must

N

not throw John's expenses on Mr. Carrysford beyond this term, and my means will not allow me to keep two boys at school at the same time. We must do the best we can with Harry, and leave results in higher hands. One circumstance connected with Harry's misconduct, Nelly, has given me a great deal of pleasure."

" O papa, what is it ? "

" To see you so patient with his faults. A few months back you would have been more ready to be angry with them than mourn over them, I think."

" Yes, papa, I know I should. But it seems so easy to be quiet and good while I lie here, and give so much trouble to everybody. Sometimes I am afraid that I shall be just as cross and impatient as ever, when I get well."

" I hope not, Nelly. But it is as well to be a little mistrustful of yourself; it will lead you to lean more entirely on Him who is able to keep you from falling."

An hour later Mr. Carrysford came in, bringing Harry, whom he had found, with two or three other boys, trespassing on his plantation. He was sent off at once to his bedroom ; but, as he looked pale and wretched, Mary was told to take him up a hot cup of tea as soon as he was in bed.

"Ah, that's how you spoil him," said Mr. Carrysford, who had overheard the direction to Mary. " A sound flogging would do him far more good !"

However, that was a mode of correction that Mr. Carrysford was far more ready to talk about than administer.

"I think punishment only hardens him," said Mr. Foster.

"Yes, that's what people always say now-a-days, and so young scapegraces get off on easy terms. Things were different when you and I were boys, and we're better men for it now, depend upon it."

"Very likely," said Mr. Foster, smiling, "but I should not like to lift my hand against a child."

"Then you must send him to school. Put him among a few good lads, and he might do well enough."

"He always did till John went away," said Ellen.

"Then John shan't go any more," remarked Master Lenny. "He must stay at home, and take care of Harry."

"Not a bad idea," said Mr. Carrysford. "And my Ned had better stay and take care of me. I miss him twenty times a day, and so does his mother. It's very hard to have to part with one's boys just as they begin to get companionable. Sometimes I think I'll try the Grants' plan, and have a tutor for them at home."

"It does not always answer," said Mr. Foster. "Boys are often idle under home tuition."

"Well, the Grants are not. You would not find better trained lads in the whole county. I should be quite satisfied if mine were only doing half as well."

"Yes, but they have an admirable master."

"Ah, that's it! If I could find such another I'd make my boys over to him to-morrow."

But Mr. Carrysford was so much given to talking in this strain whenever the holidays were near, that no one paid any attention to it now, not even Ellen, though she often thought how nice it would be for **Harry** to have Tom and Edgar Carrysford for constant neighbours.

However, when she heard a few days later that the Grants, a wealthy family in the next parish, were about to part with their tutor, as their sons were going to college, she began to hope that the long talked of plan would be carried out at last, and asked her papa if he thought it likely.

"I believe it is almost certain," replied Mr. Foster ; "but you shall hear all about it to-morrow, when John comes home."

"Why, is there anything more, papa?"

"Yes, a great deal, but you must wait and let him tell you."

It was hard to be patient under the circumstances, even till the next afternoon. But it came at last, and John was set down at the gate in the midst of even a more deafening uproar than had been raised at his departure.

"What is it, John?" were Ellen's first words, as soon as his rough greeting was over. "What have you to tell me?"

"Guess!" answered John, stretching himself on the floor at her side, and holding Lenny up at arm's length as easily as if he had been one of the sofa cushions.

"But I can't—do tell me."

"Well, I'm not going to school any more."

"O John, does papa say so?" and Ellen did not quite know whether to be glad or sorry.

"Yes, and I say so, too! The Carrysfords are going to have Mr. Chase, the Grants' old tutor, and we are to study with them."

" But will you like that, John ? "

" Why, I should think so ! See what Hector Grant's college course has been, and they say it was all owing to Mr. Chase. We shall get on famously."

Mary came in just then with the tea, so John scrambled to his feet, and busied himself with the cups and saucers as handily as if he had never left home. Mr. Foster leaned back in his easy chair, and watched him quietly. He was thinking, like Ellen, what a comfort it would be to have him at home. Only Harry looked miserable, and he scarcely dared to lift his eyes to John's pleasant face. But brighter days were coming even for him. With John and the Carrysfords for companions, he was not likely to care quite so much for the society of the Longs, or even of Snap and his master.

" Do you know that I am much better ? " whispered Ellen, as John carried her to her bedroom that night. " Sometimes I feel as if I could walk up by myself."

" Yes, I've heard about it. I called on the doctor as we passed through London, and he says I'm to let him know every week how you are. That will be getting my hand in, won't it ? "

" For what, John ? "

" Why, for doctoring. Wouldn't you like me to take up that pleasant calling ? "

" No, not at all. I want you to be a clergyman and help papa. Don't you think that would be better ? "

John answered " Yes," with unusual gravity, and then said how sorry he was to see his father looking so pale and careworn.

" Yes, he has had so much to vex him since you have been away, John. But now there seems such a bright time before 'us, that I feel half afraid when I think of it."

" Afraid of what, Nell ? "

" That its pleasantness will make me give up trying to be patient and good."

" Why, can't the effort be kept up anywhere but on a hard sofa ? "

" I don't know, John. Ah, you may laugh, but sometimes I'm afraid not, and that often makes me half dread getting well again. I suppose it's very foolish."

John understood her fears. Thoughtless as he seemed, he had at heart that earnest love for the Saviour that watches jealously against the least deviation from His law. " We must not forget what our Lord says, Nelly—'Take no thought for the morrow.'"

" But that means our temporal things, John—our food and clothes."

" And why not our spiritual ones too, as He has promised to supply both ? We know that all things work together for good to them that love Him, and you must not doubt His power to keep you in health as well as in suffering."

Mary came in, just then, with a light, and John, wishing Ellen " good-night," ran down-stairs, whistling as he went. They could still hear him, after the parlour door had closed, and Mary said, as she turned to assist Ellen, that " there had not been such a pleasant sound in the house since Master John went away ! "

LONDON : R. CLAY, SON, AND TAYLOR, PRINTERS.

Society

FOR

Promoting Christian Knowledge.

BOOKS SUITABLE FOR PRESENTS.

Most of these Works may be had in ornamental bindings, with gilt edges, at an extra charge of 3d. for 18mos.; 4d. for 12mos.; 6d. for 8vos.

	Price.	
	s.	*d.*
BIBLE PICTURE BOOK, complete, containing 96 Plates, printed in three colors. Cloth boards	5	0
In 2 Vols.:—OLD AND NEW TESTAMENT. Limp cloth . . . . *each*	2	0
BIBLE PICTURES and STORIES. In 2 Vols. With 96 Plates, printed in colors:—OLD AND NEW TESTAMENT. Extra cloth gilt . . . . *each*	7	0
BIRDS' NESTS, with 22 Colored Plates of Eggs. By the Rev. C. A. JOHNS	4	6
BOOK of TRADES, The	2	0
BRITISH BIRDS in their HAUNTS. By the Rev. C. A. JOHNS	12	0
BURNT CHILD, The	1	0
CARPENTER'S FAMILY, The. A Sketch of Village Life. By Mrs. JOSEPH LAMB (RUTH BUCK), Author of "Tom Neal," &c.	2	0
CHANNEL ISLANDS, RAMBLES among the . . .	3	0
CHAPTERS on COMMON THINGS of the SEA-SIDE. By ANNE PRATT	4	0
CHEMISTRY of CREATION	5	0
(*Fcap. 8vo.*)		

BOOKS SUITABLE FOR PRESENTS.

BOOKS SUITABLE FOR PRESENTS.

BOOKS SUITABLE FOR PRESENTS.

An Allowance of 25 per Cent. to Members.

DEPOSITORIES :

77, Great Queen Street, Lincoln's Inn Fields; 4, Royal Exchange ;
and 48, Piccadilly.

www.ingramcontent.com/pod-product-compliance
Lightning Source LLC
Chambersburg PA
CBHW020604030726
47497CB00007B/2080